A PISTOL IN GREENYARDS

A PISTOL IN GREENYARDS

Mollie Hunter

CANONGATE • KELPIES

First published 1965 by Evans Brothers Ltd.
First published in Kelpies 1988
Published In Canada by Optimum Publishing
International (1984) Inc., Montreal

Cover illustration by Alexa Rutherford

Printed in Great Britain
by Cox & Wyman Ltd, Reading, Berkshire

ISBN 0 86241 175 0

*The publishers acknowledge the financial assistance
of the Scottish Arts Council in the
publication of this volume*

CANONGATE PUBLISHING LTD
17 JEFFREY STREET, EDINBURGH EH1 1DR

The clearance of Greenyards was an actual historical event. A true account of the brutal way in which it was carried out is given in the early chapters of this book, which has been written as a salute to the memory of the people of Greenyards, and especially to that of the boys and girls who kept the look-out on Ardgay Hill.

Mollie Hunter

1 I hated the very look of him

I saw him coming along the deck of the ship towards me, and even though I owed him my life, I hated the very look of him. I would have turned away then but my sister Katrine laid hold of my sleeve and spoke sharply to me.

'Have you learned no manners in your fifteen years, Connal! You would be at the bottom of the Atlantic now, but for his doctoring of you.'

And so I stayed and said good morning as civilly as I could to Dr. Andrew Hamilton, for although the despair on me was bitter enough to have wished he had let me die, I could not shame my sister in front of such a fine Lowland gentleman.

'Ah, so you speak English as well as the native Gaelic of the Highlands,' he remarked, and if I had had the pistol with me that I had in Greenyards, I would have shot him dead for the condescension in his tone.

'I could wish,' said I bitterly, 'that I had never learned to speak the tongue of such a barbarous people.'

Katrine bit her lip at the way I spoke and Hamilton glanced at her as if to ask whether she shared my feelings. She flushed under his look and with a toss of her head moved closer to me. He smiled a little.

'I see, Miss Ross, that you are at one with your young friend in this matter. But surely you do not class a Lowland Scot like myself along with the English?'

'It was Englishmen made the laws that brought us to the pass we are in,' I answered fiercely for Katrine, 'but it is Lowland Scotsmen like yourself who have reaped the benefit of them!'

His manner changed at that, as I had thought it would. He began speaking again – fine phrases about our disobedience to the laws and our foolishness in trying to resist the march of progress, but I was too angry to stay and listen to him now, even for Katrine's sake.

'*Savages,*' he had called the poor Highland emigrants crowding the deck that morning the ship had weighed anchor for the Americas, and sick as I had been at the time, the scorn in his voice had struck sharply through the mists of fever in my brain. I had hated him then for his contempt of us, and remembering the way he had spoken had hated him anew as he came along the deck of the ship towards me. I hated him still. Why should I stay meekly and listen to him!

I turned roughly away but this time it was himself that stopped me with one hand on my arm. His grip had a surprising strength in it for such a fine white hand, and there was a snap of steel in his voice too when he said:

'*You* are the boy that pulled the pistol on the Sheriff-Officer in Greenyards. You are Connal Ross!'

He made it sound like a statement but I knew it could only be a shot at random for only my own people knew my true identity and they would never have betrayed me to this Lowlander. And yet, I was so sick by this time of hiding and running that I looked him straight in the eye and said bluntly:

'Yes. I was the one that pulled the pistol on the Sheriff-Officer.'

Katrine gave a little moan of alarm. Quickly, before Hamilton could speak, she said: 'Connal had no choice! The Officer would have killed —'

I stopped her mouth gently with my hand and turned her away from Hamilton. Too much had been said already, I realized, and to say more would only bring trouble on those who had helped me as well as on myself.

'Come, Katrine,' I commanded. 'They can arrest me if they wish when we reach the Americas. Meanwhile let us keep our pride, for it is all they have left to us.'

And Katrine, though she is a strong-willed girl and two years older than I am, did as I bid her. She dropped the briefest of curtsies to Dr. Hamilton and we left him standing there by the ship's side and staring angrily after us.

We quarrelled about Hamilton afterwards. I said he was a prying informer and Katrine said, for shame, if it had not been for his skill I would have died of the typhus and so would many of the others who had fallen sick with it. Then she added, with that little smile and sidelong glance of the eyes that females use when they are speaking of a young man, that he was a fine-looking fellow and clever, no doubt, with his doctor's degree and all.

'You are not setting your cap at *him*?' I asked her, astonished, and she flared out at me.

'Do you think I could forget sooner than you our mother lying in the gaol at Inverness or all the slaughter that took place at Greenyards? I will marry a Highlander like myself – if I marry at all!'

And so she left me to brood and feed on the black bitterness of my anger as I had been doing ever since that day she spoke of. And it was then, lying in the crowded, evil-smelling dimness of the emigrant quarters of the ship, *Good Chance*, with

9

the movement of bodies and the soft lilt of our own Gaelic language all about me, that I made up my mind to write my own account of what had happened at Greenyards. For how else could I ever make people like Andrew Hamilton understand that *my* people were not cattle to be driven hither and thither as it pleased the great ones of the world? How else could I tell the world of the injustice my people had suffered, how and why we had fought against it? And tell the world I must, if the flame of anger in me was not to consume my brain completely.

I had reached this point in my thinking when it occurred to me that I had neither pen nor paper with which to carry out my purpose. Neither had I the wherewithal to purchase them from the ship's stores. I struck the flat of my hand against the bulkhead in despair, and the jar of pain it brought my wounded shoulder laid me back, gasping, on my bunk.

That day was the first time I had had strength enough to climb to the upper deck, but the freshness of the air there had put new life in me. As the last traces of the fever left me I was able to move more and more freely round the ship, but although this meant that I saw the ship's surgeon every day at some time or another, I avoided speaking to him again. I saw Katrine in conversation with him a few times, and though I was curious to know what had passed between them she would not tell me.

Then one day as I stood leaning over the ship's side he approached me himself and stood beside me. He did not speak and the silence endured till I was forced to look sideways at him. He was a fine-looking fellow as Katrine had said – I had to admit that – very smart in a blue and buff coat with his fair hair cut neatly short above its collar and strong features ruddily-tanned by the sea-wind.

Indeed, he was the sort of young fellow I could have liked – if I had not known him for what he was. A Lowlander, a natural-born hater of the Highland people. A man from the soft, fat lands of the south who knew nothing and cared less for our hard way of life among the mountains. A man who knew nothing of the way we had been driven from our homes there.

'So Katrine Ross is your sister,' he remarked at length.

I said nothing and after another silence he added, 'You rouse my curiosity, Connal Ross. You are wanted for a crime of considerable violence, and yet you do not speak like one who lacks education.'

There was such surprise in his tone that in other circumstances I might have laughed at his ignorance of the high value we place on learning in our glen.

'I have had the education that everyone in our glen has had,' I said turning my head to him.

His eyes were on me, very keen and blue, surgeon's eyes probing for any weakness on my part, and to show him that I had not softened from our first conversation I added,'Though it was not all of us who went to the trouble of learning the English tongue. The sensible ones were content with the beauties of our own Gaelic language.'

'But you are so poor,' he said, puzzled. 'So remote in your mountains from everything we in the south understand as culture.'

'Oh, so it is culture you call it, then!' Mocking him I was, by this time. 'We have simpler names than that for telling stories and making poems.'

He went off on a different tack then, suddenly demanding to know, 'Why did the men of Greenyards run away from the battle?'

I held on to my rage, damping down the fire of it with slow, careful words.

'That was only one of the lies that were printed about us in the newspapers at the time. And if you knew my people at all,

Dr. Hamilton, you would know just how much you have been deceived by those lies.'

He turned away from me and walked some steps back and forward along the deck, frowning and biting his lip. There was a look of bewilderment on his face that told me I had cracked the hard surface of his attitude to us. I spoke again, driving the wedge of doubt deeper into his mind.

'If you did know the truth of it you would see how arrogantly you have judged us.'

'Aye. Aye,' he muttered to himself, and then suddenly he shot at me, 'I want to know the truth of it now, Connal Ross. I have had time to observe and think since you all came aboard, and I want to know how it is that such an accusation could be brought against people with the courtly manners of those in the emigrant quarters. I want to know why some of them should be suffering now from typhus fever – why so many of them have new-healed scars on their heads and shoulders —'

'They are savages – you said so yourself,' I jeered at him, but he swept on not heeding my interruption,

'– and why a pretty young woman like your sister should have the same kind of scar on her scalp as well as having been wounded by a pistol bullet.'

He had come close up to me while he was talking and laid his hand on my shoulder, but I shook it off.

'I cannot tell you,' I said roughly, 'for I could not speak of it without tears, and I am too much of a man grown now to cry like a girl.'

I turned away from him and looked seawards so that my face was hidden from him and after a minute I added quietly, 'Yet I could write it down – I *will* write it down to show everyone the truth of what happened, whenever I can get my hands on pen and paper. I can do it, I know, for I was a pupil of John Chisholm, our bard, and he trained me how to hold a story in my head so that I could pass it on to future generations.'

I had hardly finished talking before he was plucking at my sleeve and urging me along the deck with him.

'Come, boy, come!'

And then as we reached the head of a companion-way, pushing at me till I had my foot on the first step, 'Down below to my cabin!'

I did as he told me, wondering all the time what he meant to do and why I should be so weakly agreeing with his intention.

'In there,' he commanded, and I found myself inside a cabin with all the appliances of his profession displayed about it, and in the centre of it a heavy table of dark wood bolted to the deck and holding an array of writing materials.

Still guiding me by his grip on my sleeve he sat me down on a heavy swinging chair in front of the desk. My hand itched to reach out and grasp one of the pens in the silver tray there and, as if he had guessed the temptation they were to me, he picked one up and placed it by my hand.

'There,' said he. 'You have everything you need to write down what you know, and I will tell the steward that you are to have the use of my cabin at any time you may want it.'

I drew back the hand that was reaching for the pen in front of me and eyed him as coldly as the words on my tongue were hot with contempt.

'How much do you expect to be paid for the information that will lay me by the heels?'

I had thought he might strike me for this but he was so little offended that he even laughed.

'It is the Americas you sail to, Connal Ross! A big, broad country where no one will be concerned to pursue you for a crime committed in the county of Ross in Scotland!'

'We sail under the English flag,' I countered. 'You could still have me arrested aboard ship and sent back to stand trial in Inverness.'

He was still amused and showed it as he said, 'I am passing

well off as a doctor, boy. I have no need to earn a few dirty coppers by spying – but nevertheless, we will make a safeguard against any sudden urge on my part to earn Judas-money. You need not show me what you have written until we are both on American soil. Does that satisfy you?'

Still I hesitated. I could not understand how it was that the contempt of my people which had made me hate him had turned suddenly to such interest in them, and I had to know why this was before I accepted any favours from him. I told him so bluntly, and the eagerness in his face gave way to a sad and purposeful look.

'I want to know what happened at Greenyards and I want to know why it happened,' he said slowly, 'because I have a feeling that, in some far corner of my country, an injustice has been done. And, Lowlander as I am, I am still a Scot. That injustice, therefore, has been done to my people and in my name.'

His eyes held mine gravely for a moment and then he smiled suddenly, a wide and somewhat wicked grin that reminded me of the piratical features of my father's red-haired brother, Rory.

'A Lowland Scot is a stubborn creature, Connal Ross,' he said, 'and in the pursuit of truth especially there is no one can be as stubborn as a Lowland medical man. Will you take my bargain, therefore, and write?'

I tried to grasp at the skirts of the hatred I felt for him, but somehow in the past few moments it had melted away, leaving me with a shamefaced knowledge that the man was sincere in what he said. As courteously as I could, accordingly, I said: 'I accept the hospitality of your cabin and your desk, Dr. Hamilton, and I thank you for them. And I take your bargain that I will show you what I have written when we are both on American soil and I am safe from English law.'

He nodded. 'Good, good! To your labours then!' And

with another of his wide grins and an encouraging slap on the shoulder he left me sitting there.

I picked up the pen, wondering where I should begin the tale. And maybe because I had thought of him a few moments before there flashed into my mind a memory of my uncle Rory – Rory Ruadh, as he was known to all of us from the colour of his hair and beard. I saw him suddenly as he was on the day he rode into our glen carrying the news that spelt death for some of us and ruin for us all, and I realized that the moment I had caught sight of him then was the true beginning of the story I had to tell.

And so I bent my head to the paper and began to write of that moment and of the events that sprang from it, exactly as I remembered them.

2 *The four-footed clansmen have come*

The date of that day will always be burned in my mind – Wednesday, the 1st of March, 1854.

It was afternoon and I was down at the side of the River Carron cutting willow switches to make the kind of basket we use for trapping trout when I first caught sight of Red Rory riding towards me. I waved my arm to him and called out the greeting of our people.

'*Failte duibh, Rory Ruadh! Sith gun rob so!* – Welcome to you, Red Rory! Peace be here!'

Rory made no answer but kept his pony at a fast trot up the glen. I ran to meet him, puzzled by his silence, and saw that the beast he rode was all lathered with sweat and blowing hard. I seized its bridle and Rory bent to me a face as bleak as a winter hillside.

'Here, boy, you that has the great command of the English tongue,' he said. 'Read that!' And he thrust at me the newspaper he was holding in his hand.

It was folded open at a page of advertisements. I saw the date at the top of the page (nearly a week old, the paper was) and then Rory stabbed a forefinger down on one of the advertisements.

'Read it!' he urged. 'Read it out loud!'

FARMS TO LET ON THE ESTATE OF GREENYARDS IN

STRATHCARRON

The bold black type of the advertisement's heading seemed to leap out of the page at me. I read aloud:

'The Sheep-walk of Greenyards presently possessed by Mr. Alexander Munro.

'The above farms will be let on Leases of such duration as may be agreed upon, with entry at the term of Whitsunday, 1854. Further particulars will be communicated by James F. Gillanders, Esq., Highfield, by Beauly, to whom offers are to be addressed.'

'I cannot believe it!' I lifted my head from the paper, staring up at Red Rory and repeating, 'I *cannot* believe it!'

'No one has ever been able to believe it at first,' Rory Ruadh said harshly, 'but there you have it in cold print and so it must be true. Our farms are to be taken from us, boy. The four-footed clansmen have come at last to Greenyards!'

He kicked heels to the sides of his poor exhausted beast to urge it on. I ran alongside him and together we continued up the glen. Ahead of us lay the scattered farms with the houses of the families who shared their ownership grouped in the centre of each. 'Townships' we called these groups of dwellings and to each of them, we knew, the news of the advertisement must be brought as quickly as possible.

It had been a long time coming, I thought as I ran beside the pony. Forty years now, our people had lived in dread of it, for the invasion of the Lowland graziers with their great herds of sheep – 'the four-footed clansmen' as the people had bitterly named them – had been going on all that time. One by one the chiefs of the clans who had lived in the glens since time immemorial had discovered the profits to be made from wool and mutton and had rented their lands to the southern graziers.

17

One by one the glens on all sides of us had been cleared of people to make way for sheep. And now it was our turn to be turned out of our farms, as thousands had been before us, to die of hunger or to be driven miserably into exile in the Americas.

I looked up at Rory with a cry of protest against the injustice of it ready to spring to my lips, but his mouth was tight set, his eyes narrowed to peer forward at the houses we were nearing. It was not a face to invite speech and so I kept my words to myself.

It was our own township we were approaching and Rory's trained soldier's sight caught the flutter of a kerchief at the byre door before I noticed anything moving there.

'The women are back from the milking,' he said. 'There will be plenty of tongues to spread the word around now,' and he urged the pony even faster.

It was my sister Katrine he had seen. She came running to meet us, her red shawl tumbling off the cloudy dark mass of her hair, her feet in their little deerskin shoes skimming swallow-quick over the hillside's great tussocks of coarse grass.

'Rory! Rory Ruadh!' she was calling. 'Did you find me any of the bonnie red ribbon you promised to look for in Inverness?'

'You tell her,' Rory said. 'I will go on and break the news to your mother and grandfather.'

I caught Katrine and steadied her as she fetched up, laughing, against the pony's side. Rory touched his hand lightly to her cheek, then he was off and she was brushing my hands away and scolding at me to know the cause of the mystery. I hushed her down. She has courage, my sister, and so I did not try to spare her. I read the advertisement out exactly as it stood in the paper.

Katrine said nothing when I had finished. She just stood there staring at me, her eyes wide open with shock and all the

18

fresh colour draining out of her face. Her lips trembled a little and then she stammered,

'Can we – could we not offer Gillanders more rent for our land?'

'We can never offer him the money he would make from sheep. You know that, Katrine.'

I turned her by the shoulders and faced her up the glen. 'Look! See the green pastures of it – see how sheltered it is! He will get a high price for it as a sheep-walk – far higher than any rents our little farms can afford to pay.'

'But, Connal, where can we go if we are turned out?' You would have thought for the moment that I was the older of the two the way she was appealing to me. 'There is no other land to be had – the sheep have taken it all! We will have no money except what we can get for the stock —'

'– and that will be little enough!' I finished for her. 'Gillanders will buy it at valuation price – *his* valuation, and that will not bring more than a few pounds to each family in the glen. There is little or no market for our cattle in the south now that the French wars are over.'

'We must write to our father! He will tell Major Robertson – get him to order Gillanders not to put us out!'

She went on talking, her face suddenly so alight with the new idea that I hardly had the heart to stop her. And yet I had to for, though Major Robertson, our laird, and my father were soldiering in the same regiment far away in Australia, I knew that a foot-soldier like him would be powerless against the wishes of his officer. And knowing my father, I knew also that he would not stay dumb under this treatment to his family so that nothing but trouble for him could result from our writing.

I told her as gently as I could, 'Katrine, Gillanders is only the factor for the estate of Greenyards so that he could not be proposing to turn us out now unless he had already received direct instructions from Major Robertson to do so. It would be no use appealing against such an instruction, Katrine. You know as well as I do that the Major is southern born and bred for all that he bears a Highland name. He has never even seen Greenyards and he neither knows nor cares what goes on here so long as Gillanders administers the estate well enough to keep him supplied with money.'

'I cannot believe it! I cannot believe it!'

She was like I had been myself, now, repeating her bewilderment over and over again.

'Connal, there have been families of Ross and Munro in this glen for five hundred years! The glen belongs to us, Connal – they cannot turn us out after all that time!'

'They can do it in law – but whether they can do it in fact ...'

I left the sentence unfinished, hardly knowing what I meant by it, but thinking somehow of the expression of bitter determination on Red Rory's face. We stood staring at one another and Katrine said abruptly:

'There will be a meeting at the schoolhouse tonight.'

I nodded and pointed to the figures already hurrying between the different townships. There was bound to be a meeting that night as soon as everyone had received word of the advertisement, but the glen was wide and the townships were scattered. It would take time for them all to gather. Meanwhile, the urge was strong on me to talk with old John Chisholm, our blind bard – Blind John, as we called him. I felt that I wanted nothing so much at that moment as to hear the old man talk of the five hundred years of history the men of my name had made in the glen. Besides, I could help him down to the meeting later on.

'Go home now and see to the supper with mother,' I told Katrine. 'I will go and fetch Blind John down to the meeting.'

She smiled a little, knowing my fondness for the old man and that this was a roundabout way of saying that I wanted to talk with him, and all at once became my older sister again.

'See that you are in time for your supper then,' she ordered. 'And bring the old man with you when you come for it.'

I told her that I would bring him to sit down with us. Then I left her and hurried up the rise to the cottage where John Chisholm lived, looking ahead all the time to see if I could catch sight of him sitting at the door of it. This was his favourite place, the old stone bench outside his door where he could sit with the sun warm on his blind eyes and feel the air of the glen on his face.

I saw him there as I topped the rise, his white hair lifting a little from his head in the breeze and his hand up shading his eyes as if they could see. I called out to him but he did not drop his hand or call back to me, and I felt a sudden chill run over me for there was something strange in his silence and in the intent peering towards me of his sightless face. I stopped in front of him, hesitating whether or not to greet him again, but before I could speak the old man said in a high, strained voice:

'Katrine ... Katrine Ross ...'

'Katrine is not with me – it is Connal Ross who is here,' I said, but as if I had not spoken at all he went on speaking in the same strange way,

'Katrine, my little dove, why is there blood running down your face?'

'John – Blind John —' I began, but the old man interrupted me, stumbling to his feet and crying out:

'Watch out for his pistol, Connal – he is going to shoot!'

I whirled round in the direction his hand was pointing but there was no one there, nothing but the bare hillside all round us. A moaning sound brought me whipping back to the blind man again in time to see him slide to the ground in a faint. Then I knew that he had had a vision and that the words he had spoken had to do with what had taken place in his vision, for Blind John had the second-sight. Many a time he had seen into the future and what he had seen had always come to pass, and knowing this I could do nothing for the moment but stand gaping at him lying stretched out there on the ground.

Katrine with blood on her face – someone pointing a pistol at me! What terrible thing could he have seen in his vision?

I bent over him trying to bring him to his senses but he seemed to be in some sort of seizure that had paralysed his power of speech and movement. In the end I saw that there was nothing I could do except to carry him down to our own house where my mother could take charge of him. I hoisted him on my back without too much difficulty since I am strong and broad-built for my years and his frame was thin and frail with age. Then I carried him down to the township, stepping gently so as to cause him as little pain as possible.

I must confess, however, that my thoughts as I staggered on with him were not so much with the old man's condition as with what he had said. Katrine was to be hurt in some way and I was to be threatened with a pistol. So he had seen in his vision. And was it not most likely, I argued to myself, that these things would come about as a consequence of the event that lay ahead of us – our threatened eviction from the glen?

It seemed all the more likely to me when I recalled what I had been told by people old enough to have seen for themselves the merciless way in which other glens had been cleared to make way for sheep, and with every step I took my conviction on the matter grew stronger. But if it were to be so, I vowed, I would not stand by tamely when the time came and let these things happen to Katrine and myself.

There was a pistol hidden in the thatch of heather on our house. It had been my great-great-grandfather's when he fought for Prince Charles at the battle of Culloden, and when the Disarming Act making it a criminal offence for Highlanders to own firearms was passed in 1747, he had hidden it there rather than give it up to the Sheriff-Officers who came round collecting the forbidden weapons. My grandfather had told me of this when I was a small boy – had even taken the pistol from its hiding-place and showed me that it was in working order. Then he had put it back in the thatch saying that there it must stay as a sign of the independent fighting spirit that had put it there.

I made up my mind to get that pistol out of the thatch that very night, so that I could carry it on me – just in case I should need it when the Sheriff-Officer arrived in Greenyards with the writs of eviction.

3 I will give them action!

Katrine met me on the doorstep of our house. She cried out to those within when she saw my burden, and Rory and my grandfather came hurrying to take Blind John from me. They carried him through to the inner room with my mother fussing and clucking behind them. She and Katrine stayed with him but Rory and my grandfather came quickly out again and Rory said to me:

'I am going now to see Alexander Munro at Braelangwell, Connal. I want you to come with me.'

I gaped at him. 'What would you be needing *me* for?'

'You know the position about the land, Connal.'

As he spoke, Rory began to strip off the Army uniform he had worn on his leave up till that moment and to put on some farming clothes of my father's.

'Major Robertson owns it, and Gillanders administers it for him. Alexander Munro is the tacksman, the tenant-in-chief, and our leases are only sub-leases of the main one held by him. Gillanders can therefore only evict us from our farms in order to rent the glen to southern graziers *provided* he has come to some arrangement with Munro.

'Now' – he turned to me, fastening the massive silver buckle of his uniform belt over my father's old breeches – 'Munro has said nothing to us of selling out his lease. Yet here we have the proof that the land we sub-lease from him is being advertised for a sheep-walk. How does that come to be?'

'Munro is a smooth-tongued cheat who says one thing and thinks another,' my grandfather answered bitterly for me.

'That is why you are coming with me, Connal,' Rory said, pushing me ahead of him to the door. 'Munro speaks the Gaelic as well as you or I, but a fine gentleman like him will not admit to such a lowly accomplishment. He will insist on speaking in English and you know that, for all my years in the Army, my tongue is clumsy in that language. But you have as good or better English to your tongue than he has and so you will be quick to find out any double meaning in what he says.'

We were out of the house now and striding across the heather to Braelangwell, half a mile away.

'We must pin him down, boy, pin him down,' Rory went on. 'If he has made a secret arrangement with Gillanders, the writs of eviction will be signed by him and so they will have the full force of the law. But if Gillanders has acted over his head – if he has not signed writs against us and does not mean to – then we are protected against the law. For the time being, at any rate.'

We strode on in silence till it struck me suddenly that the paper with the advertisement in it had not been a Highland one. Its title, I remembered, had been the *Berwickshire Gazette*.

'How did you happen on the advertisement in the first place?' I asked curiously.

'I got it from a drover in Inverness,' Rory told me. 'He was not exactly sober when I met up with him, and after I had plied him with more whisky he babbled enough to let me know he had been sent up from the south to look over some land that had been advertised for a sheep-walk. And he said, moreover, that he had been well warned not to let his business be known to anyone in the north! I left him sleeping, the whisky having overcome him by that time, but first I prised the paper gently out of his hand and brought it back with me.'

He gave an exasperated tug at the jacket he was wearing. 'This is too tight,' he complained. 'Your father is not so broad as I am.'

'Then why wear it?' I asked, and impatiently he answered, 'Use the brains God gave you, boy! No one knows which way the cat will jump from now on, and if I should happen to be found on the wrong side of the law things would go doubly hard with me if I was in uniform at the time.'

I remembered then that a serving soldier who was found guilty of a civil offence had to submit to being tried and punished by the Army also, once he had served the sentence passed on him by a civilian court. And remembering also a description my father had once given me of the brutality of Army punishment, I walked on beside Rory wondering uneasily just what sort of situation he foresaw that put him in danger of having *his* back flogged to raw flesh while the Drum-Major counted the strokes.

As it happened on that occasion, however, my fears for Rory were unfounded – as were his own misgivings that he might be misled by Munro's smooth tongue. The tacksman received us affably, and when Rory challenged him with the advertisement his round, smooth face showed only surprise and concern.

'This thing has been done without my knowledge, Rory Ruadh,' he said solemnly, 'and I do assure you that I have not authorized anyone to issue writs of eviction in my name.'

It was hard to doubt a statement made with such seriousness. I found myself looking away from the plump little man, so fashionably dressed and so much at ease in his fine white-panelled study, and feeling more than a little foolish at ever having suspected him of double-dealing.

'It is myself that is pleased to hear you say so, Mr. Munro,' Rory said, 'for, as you well know, we cannot be legally evicted without your consent in writing.'

'I think you can take it that I am sufficiently acquainted with the law to realize that.'

Munro's tone was a trifle sharper now but Rory pressed on nevertheless, 'You understand then how important it is for the people to be assured of your support if they decided to resist any attempt at evicting them. Will you give us your word on what you have said, Mr. Munro? Will you swear before your Maker that you have not signed any writs against us?'

'If you wish it.'

Munro rose from behind his elegant desk and straightened up with a tolerant half-smile on his face. He raised his right hand and said:

'I swear before my Maker that I have not authorized anyone to issue writs in my name against the people of Greenyards.'

Rory caught my eye, nodding his satisfaction at this declaration. It seemed a perfectly straightforward one to me and we took our leave of him with handshakes of goodwill on either side. A serving-girl showed us to the front door – a different one from the girl who had ushered us into the study to wait for Munro. This girl was Jean Chisholm by name, a great-niece of Blind John, and so I seized the chance to let her know what had happened to the old man and to reassure her that we were looking after him. I thought that she looked at me rather strangely while I was speaking and when we reached the front door I found the reason for this.

With her hand on the latch and a quick glance behind her to make sure there was no one but ourselves to hear she said rapidly, 'A good deed for a good deed, Connal. I was in the drawing-room making up the fire when Janet announced you to the master. He looked put out when he heard who was calling on him and then he said to the mistress, *"If this matter is what I think it is, I must ride to see Donald Stewart tonight." '*

There was no time for her to say more. Munro's voice calling to her came from along the passage and she left us looking at one another in dismay, for Donald Stewart, in the town of Tain, fifteen miles off, was Munro's law-agent – as we both well knew.

'Do you think he means to go back on his word?' I asked Rory as we stepped out for home, but Rory would not venture an opinion.

'It is too early to tell,' was all he would say when I pressed him, and then he warned me, 'Say nothing of this, Connal, except to your mother and grandfather, till we have more evidence one way or another. It will only confuse matters if it is generally talked about just now.'

That was the end of the matter till we reached home, but my mother would not let it rest so easily. She served supper for us, listening to what Rory had to say, and then she turned to my grandfather with the remark:

'It seems you were right then about Munro, Donald Ban.'

'It is a solemn oath he has sworn,' he told her. 'Give him the benefit of the doubt, Anne.'

'It is us that will need any benefits that are going if Munro has lied!' she flashed back at him.

Katrine and the men glanced at one another in silence for my mother is a formidable woman to argue with when her mind is made up on anything. Moreover, her judgment is usually very shrewd and they were well aware of this. Katrine rose and went back to the inner room where Blind John lay. My mother rolled down the sleeves of her dress and fastened the cuffs, and as she moved to take her shawl off its hook on the door she said:

'Make haste with your supper, Connal. It is time we were off to the meeting.'

I had been dawdling with my food, hoping I might be left behind to finish it when they went out.

'Do not wait for me,' I told her hastily. 'I want to look in on Blind John, in any case, before I go.'

She sighed. 'You can do nothing for him, son. It is a stroke he has suffered and all we can do is wait for him to come out of it. Katrine will watch him tonight while we are out.'

'I will just bring in more peats to make a good fire for her then before I follow you,' I said, and the three of them went out without noticing that the basket of peats by the fire was still more than half full.

As soon as the door closed behind them I dragged the table over till it rested beneath the pistol's hiding-place. I placed a chair on top and climbing on to it thrust my hand deep into the heather laid over the roof-beams. My fingers gripped the pistol. I pulled it out and then explored the place where it had rested in case there were any more weapons hidden there. This time my find was a leather pouch of powder and ball. It was more than I had dared hope for and I jumped down exulting in my luck.

I had no fear of Katrine coming on me while I did all this. I knew I could trust her not to speak of it if she had discovered me – though I would not have told her of Blind John's vision or that I wanted the pistol because of it. There was no need for her to be frightened before she had to be.

I took no care, therefore, to be quiet in my movements when I pulled the table out and then replaced it. In spite of that, there was still no sign of life from the inner room in the few moments it took for me to load the pistol, and so I stuck it into my belt, thrust the ammunition pouch deep into my breeches pocket and went quickly from the house.

It was dark outside now, and cold, with a sharp little wind

29

blowing down from the corries – the deep rock-fissures that seamed the higher stretches of the valley's mountain-face. I stood for a moment to accustom my eyes to the gloom, then I buttoned my jacket over the pistol and made off in the direction of the torches flaring round the dark outline of the school-house.

All paths in the glen led to the school-house that night. Figures loomed out of the dark on every side of me as I hurried towards it. I heard voices calling and being answered by others and well before I reached the school-house I fell in with a party that had several young fellows of my own age in it. There was Murdo Ross and the twin brothers Ewan and Donald Munro, and Murdo's cousin, Angus Ross, who was two years older than the others, and moments later we met with Lachlan Chisholm who was in his second year as a student of medicine at Glasgow University and only home in the glen for the Easter holidays.

We all kept together, running ahead of the children and the older people, and worked our way to the front of the crowd already gathered in front of the school-house. They were going to hold the meeting outside, it seemed – indeed, they could never have got that crowd, a hundred and fifty all told, into our little schoolroom.

The master's desk was set outside in front of the door. Mr. Aird, our minister, was sitting behind it, and by his side stood Rory Ruadh with the flaring light from a great knot of wood held high in his hand. More light came from lanterns gleaming and bobbing in the crowd and, like their shifting gleam breaking up the darkness, snatches of the crowd's conversation came fitfully to me out of the steady murmur of their voices.

'. . . the terrible laws the English government has made against us . . .'

That was from a woman with a shawl drawn tight round an old, wrinkled face.

'. . . and us sending our men-folk to fight for them in their wars against the French . . .'

'Three brothers I had that died in the French wars . . .'

That was another old woman answering her, her voice keening as sad as the winter wind over the snow in the corries:

'. . . three brothers, three bonny brothers. And now they are dead, the fine young men are all dead . . .'

I felt a shiver go up my spine as the wailing voices of the cailleachs, the old women, sounded in my ears. I looked around me, realizing with sudden dismay how the old people and the children outnumbered those in their thirties and forties, and how greatly also the women outnumbered the men.

It could not be otherwise, of course, for it has always been our way of life that the men should go soldiering in their young days while their families cared for the land till their return. In the old days they had fought only for their chief, acknowledging no higher allegiance. But those days were dead. Nowadays it was the government and not the chief who ruled in the Highlands, yet still our young men went soldiering in the clan-regiments the government raised when it needed fighting-men.

Six hundred of them they had raised from Greenyards and the other little glens of Strathcarron to fight in the war against the French Napoleon, six hundred young men all under twenty years old. And of that six hundred, five hundred and eighty-nine had been killed. So there we stood that cold March evening, a people who had lost a generation from among them – a generation that would have bred strong sons to be our shield at that moment! But instead of that, I thought looking around me, we had only old men like my grandfather, boys like Murdo and Ewan and myself, and a few – a very few men of an age and with a will to fight.

I shivered again, thinking of the bonny fighting-men who had died, for suddenly it seemed to me that the mountainside must be thronging with the quiet ghosts of them, and they sad for us in the useless glory of their valiant death.

I should have been listening to Mr. Aird, of course. He had opened the meeting with prayer as was the rule at any gathering in the glen, for in all things it is our custom earnestly to apply the Word of God to our lives. I had been so taken up with my thoughts, however, that I heard only the tail-end of what he said and I bowed my head hastily for the Amen hoping that none of the Elders of the church had marked my fall from grace.

Mr. Aird followed his prayer up with a short speech setting out the facts of the case. Rory must have told him of our visit to Munro for he mentioned that we had gone to see the tacksman and had got his assurance that he would not be a party to our eviction. Our position was sound in law, therefore, he assured us, and he would speak to that point later in the meeting. Then he called on my grandfather, as the leading Elder of the church, to speak to the people.

My grandfather stepped forward, holding himself so erect for all his sixty-eight years, that the men around him looked small beside his great height. Donald Ban – Donald of the fair hair, they had named him in his youth, but now his hair, which he wore flowing on to his shoulders in the old style, was white. And with this and the long white beard of him, he looked like a prophet out of the Old Testament. Like a prophet too, he spoke in a loud, ringing voice of the death and doom and destruction that had followed the coming of the sheep to the Highlands.

'There is no need to tell my own generation or my sons' generation of this,' he cried, 'for they have seen it all with their own eyes! It is our grandsons and grand-daughters – you young people there who are not yet twenty years of age and so are too young to have seen an eviction, who must realize how things will be if we allow this to happen to us. Understand now, my children, if we are driven from this glen there will be nowhere for us to go but beyond the seas! The sheep-walks are all round us now. Our little glen is one of the last where people have been allowed to live in the old way and so there is no other land for us. Homeless, because our houses will be burned by the Sheriff's men, landless because we will be driven out of our farms, we will suffer the fate that thousands of Highlanders have already suffered. Starvation or exile will be our choice!

'The cities of the south have nothing to offer us for we have no skill in city crafts – and even those of you who could reach a city and find employment there would find yourselves suffocating in the smoke and dirt of its filthy air. You might manage to survive such a life, but even if you did – you young people who have been brought up in the admonition of the Lord to respect your parents and to care for the sick and the aged – you could do so only at the expense of the helpless ones you would leave behind you.'

So still were the people listening to him that there was not even the sound of grass or heather-stems rustling underfoot. It seemed to me that we were held to him by some invisible bond and, as if he sensed the pull of it between us, my grand-father gave a tug on it then that sent shivers running up my back.

'It is more than our homes they would take from us,' he cried. 'It is the heritage to which we have been born and which has been ours for generation upon generation, so that now it is only in the high, pure air of mountains that our spirits can breathe! Out of sight of them we would sicken and die with longing for the feel of heather under our feet, for the sight of bracken glinting in the sun, and for the sound of rivers rushing down between the stones! We old people would sicken and die, and even you young people would never cease to feel the ache of longing in your hearts, for the tall mountains and the green

33

valleys between them are as much home to the Highlander as is the roof over his head. I, Donald Ban, who have wandered the world over soldiering in many countries, do tell you this now. If you leave Greenyards you will wake many a night, weeping. And wondering why there should be such a fierce ache of pain in your hearts will know such bitterness of sorrow as comes only to those who have been driven forth, never to return, from the glen of their fathers.'

The great roll of his voice ceased. There was a moment's silence that was broken by a voice crying, 'It is true! Donald Ban has spoken the bitter truth!' then they all pressed forward on him shouting that they would die rather than leave the glen. Some wept, and some were so moved by his words that they seized his hand and kissed it. I caught a sudden sight of Margaret Munro, Katrine's best friend, with her hands clasped to her breast, her head thrown back, eyes closed and tears streaming down her upturned face. The lads beside me were wild with excitement, jumping up and down and shouting:

'We will not go, Donald Ban! We will not go! No one shall drive us from our home!'

The cailleachs beside me were babbling of other evictions; of Strathnaver, where they had not waited till the people were out before they fired the houses so that old people and children had been caught in the flames; of Glencalvie, where the only shelter the people could find on the stormy night of their eviction was the lee of the churchyard wall.

I said nothing and I did not move. I could not, for the life of me, for the knowledge was on me stronger than it had ever been before that my feet were on the soil which had been trodden by those of my blood for five hundred years. My feet were rooted to it, it seemed to me then, as deeply as the heather that grew there. And in the wonder and pride of that moment, I was speechless.

34

Rory began calling for quiet at last, and when the people were once more ready to listen, Mr. Aird spoke to them again.

'It is one thing to say you will not leave the glen,' said he, 'and another thing to prevent that happening! Your legal position is strong, of course, so long as you have the support of Mr. Munro. Furthermore, I cannot believe that Major Robertson would countenance the clearance if he realized what it means to the people. He is, after all, a gentleman, and brought up to respect the feelings of others.'

There was a little murmur at this which showed that other people shared my doubts about Major Robertson. Mr. Aird ignored it and went on:

'It is impossible to approach Major Robertson in time to do any good, of course, but I shall do what I can in other directions for I am convinced that if the public at large had been aware of the extent and cruelty of the evictions which have already taken place, there would have been an outcry against them. It is my intention, therefore, to muster as much public support as possible for our cause, in particular by letting it be known through the great newspapers of the south how we are placed. Thus we may hope to stay the hand of the Sheriff from enforcing any writs that are issued. But this will all take time, and so your energies must now be bent to obtaining that time for yourselves.'

Apart from that first little murmur of doubt, no one thought of questioning this intention of Mr. Aird's for, though still only a young man, he was highly respected in the glen for his learning and for the sincerity of his nature. One burly fellow however, Ian Mackenzie by name, called out:

'We are quite willing to play for time, Mr. Aird, if we know how to go about it. But how are we to do this?'

'I will tell you!' Rory Ruadh shouted, and stepped forward confidently with the flaring branch held high and lighting his face for everyone to see.

'Donald Ban has spoken to the young people. He gave them words, strong and truthful words to move their hearts. Now I will give them action for their hands!'

He pointed his torch to the group where I stood and called to us, 'Connal! Donald! Ewan! All you young lads step forward. And the rest of you young people, girls as well as boys, come here also to me. Step back now if you please, the cailleachs and the bodachs, and let the young people through!'

The old men – the bodachs – and the old women stood aside for all the young people coming forward to answer Rory's call. I went with them, my heart pounding with excitement now at the prospect of action, and I could tell from the faces of the boys and girls jostling me that the blood was running as hot in their veins as it was in mine. We gathered in a close group round Rory Ruadh, watching as he began rapidly to chalk in the outlines of a map on the smooth top of the master's desk, talking to us all the time as he did so.

4 Do any of you doubt such an oath?

'Here,' said Rory, 'here is our glen running from east to west, inland from the sea-coast. Here is the River Carron running down its centre, and here on the north and south banks of the river lies the estate of Greenyards, four miles from the eastern end of the glen.'

He looked round to see that we were all following him and then went on: 'The Sheriff's Officer may come either from Tain to the south-east of us or from Inverness, due south of the glen. But, from whichever town he comes, the only road he can take into the glen is visible for miles from the summit of Ardgay Hill – here, at the eastern end of the glen. You have grasped this?'

We all chorused our understanding and he raised his voice so that the older people surrounding our group could hear him.

'Now then, here is what we can do to resist the delivery of the writs. The young people will take turns to stand day and night watch on Ardgay Hill along with two or three men like myself. The men will have muskets – we all know there are some still hidden in the thatch of various houses – and the young people will have whistles. We will take the schoolmaster's spy-glass for better identification of anyone approaching the glen, and at the first glimpse of a Sheriff-Officer the muskets will be fired.

'The echo of the shots will carry right up the glen. They will be the first warning and it will be followed by a chain of whistle-blasts from the young people strung out in position along the shoulder of the hill. As soon as this warning sounds the rest of you people here must make the greatest haste possible down to the eastern boundary of Greenyards. There you will have the River Carron, which is deep in that part, running close to the left-hand side of the road, and on your right hand will be the sudden rise of the hill of Cairn Mhor. Stand close together there and you will block the entry of the Sheriff-Officer into the townships.'

'But remember, no violence!' Mr. Aird broke in warningly. 'There must be no bloodshed or they will call in troops against you as they have done against others who resisted eviction!'

'What shall we do then if they come in large numbers? How can we hold the road but by force?' one man shouted, and another answered him, 'Talk sense, man! Even with the will to fight we have not enough men of an age to give them battle!'

'They will not come in any numbers till they realize that we *are* prepared to resist,' Rory shouted. 'But if and when they do it will be only for the one purpose and that will be to try and drive us out of the glen. And that they must never do, for once we are out there will be no hope of returning for us. Therefore, to gain the time we need for Mr. Aird to rouse public feeling on our behalf, we must meet their force with strategy.'

He paused, with a look around to make sure they were all marking his words well, and then explained: 'When the time comes that we see a large force approaching we will keep up a continuous musket-fire instead of firing shots only at the beginning of the warning. When you hear the sound of these continuing shots, the women *only* will gather to block the road, and by persuasion and argument they will hold back the advance of the Sheriff's men as long as possible. While they are doing this the men will be taking charge of the retreat of all the inhabitants of the townships to the higher reaches of the glen.

'We will start now carrying away stocks of food for this purpose, and when the time comes the men will carry the young children and the sick and drive the stock ahead of them to these higher reaches. For the summer is coming, my friends, and we will be able to hold out there for months yet even without roofs over our heads. Gillanders will never succeed in renting the glen for sheep so long as it is encumbered with our presence, and so will we continue to gain the time that we need to fight our cause.'

'How long will we have to get the children and the stock clear away, Rory?' Ian Mackenzie called. 'What length of warning can you give?'

'About an hour, depending on the visibility from the hill at the time,' Rory told him. 'The farthest off we can hope to sight them is four miles or so away from Ardgay Hill and after that they will have to ride round the side of the hill itself and then cover the four miles to the townships. Work it out for yourself. They will not attempt to push their horses at more than ten miles an hour over these roads. After that it is up to the women to hold the Sheriff-Officer in parley for as long as possible.'

There was a brief silence while they considered this, then a babble of talk and argument broke out. Some of the men objected that Rory's plan meant leaving the women to face any danger there might be, but the women themselves dismissed this idea.

'How can there be danger for us if there is to be no fighting?' one of them asked scornfully. The others laughed with her and argued with the men, pointing out how much fitter they were for the tasks of carrying burdens and driving the stock up steep hillsides. 'Our part is the easy one,' they maintained, and there was another burst of laughter as one of them added, 'All we have to do is to stand and talk!'

Once this had been settled some of the people were strong for putting the plan into action, but others maintained there was no need for it since Munro's assurance safeguarded us from eviction. The balance was held by those who argued that, whatever happened, it was best to be prepared for it, and it was this argument that won them all over to Rory's side in the end.

There was little need for the torches and lanterns by this time for the moon had swung clear of the cloud-wrack high overhead. It was a full moon, a great yellow moon slowly flooding the glen with silver light and casting sharp black shadows. It would give us a clear view from the top of Ardgay Hill, I thought, supposing we were to lie in wait there to see if Munro returned from Tain that night. As if he had shared this idea, Rory glanced upwards at the same time as I did and announced:

'Since you are all agreed then, we will start setting the watch this very night. You young ones, scatter now till each of you has laid hands on a whistle and meet me again at the boundary as quickly as you can.'

I remembered Katrine then, and pushing my way through the crowd till I found my mother I begged her to come home with me and release Katrine from her watch over Blind John so that she could share the excitement of the watch on the hill.

'The women must do their share in this, after all,' I pointed out and she promised, laughing.

'You and Katrine do your share on the hill and the Sheriff will have me to answer to at the boundary when he comes with his writs!'

He would and all, I thought to myself. There were not

many men who could stand up to my mother in a righteous rage! I had the sense not to say this to her, however, for though my mother is a kindly person and fond of me she is not slow to clout my ear when I am forward with my opinions.

Katrine was as eager to be off as myself when we told her the news, and while she got her shawl I found a whistle each for us and strung them on cords to hang round our necks. Then we ran as quickly as we could to the meeting-place at the boundary of Greenyards. Other boys and girls came to meet us from all directions as we ran along the road by the river, and when we were all gathered eventually there were nearly thirty of us at the meeting-place that night.

The oldest of us was Lachlan Chisholm who was nineteen and the youngest was twelve-year-old Elizabeth Ross, and with all the talk and laughter that went on as we waited for stragglers to arrive you would have thought we were going to a fair instead of to watch out for the approach of an enemy. It is very hard to be serious all the time when you are young, of course, and maybe it was because Rory remembered this that he allowed the noise to go on for a little while before he brought us back to order again.

There were another three men with him, one of them the Ian Mackenzie who had asked all the questions at the meeting. The brothers John and Peter Ross were the other two and all four of them carried muskets. They looked very military, standing with their muskets at the slope, and once Rory had quietened us he made it clear that the whole plan was to be carried out in the same military manner.

'Get into line,' he ordered us. 'Boys and girls alternately.'

We did so and then he split us into two groups with boys and girls distributed more or less evenly between them. Each group was told to number off and when this had been done, 'You will be the day watch,' he instructed the group in which I found myself, 'with myself and Ian Mackenzie for your musket-men.

Peter and John Ross here are the musket-men for this other group, the night-watch. Now, fall in behind your musket-men and march to the hill. As we climb it I will give each member of the night-watch his position, ending with the look-out man at the summit. Each person's opposite number on the day-watch will note that position so that he can take it up when his turn comes at dawn. And remember, the whistles you carry on you are to be sounded only in the event of an alarm. Any boy or girl blowing a whistle except in response to the sound of a musket-shot from higher up the hill will be severely disciplined. Do you understand?'

He gazed round us sternly while he said this, and we glanced at one another, suddenly very aware of the new importance that rested on these toys of an idle hour's wood-whittling.

There was no more talk from us after that for we had to save our breath to keep up with the fast pace Rory set along the road. It was the regulation marching-pace of a Highland Brigade, and I wondered to myself just how long the girls would keep it up without complaining. I could have saved my curiosity, however. The girls stepped shoulder to shoulder with us all the way along the road, and when we left it to climb the long shoulder of rising ground that led to the summit of the hill they kirtled up their long skirts and leapt as nimbly as we did from one piece of broken ground to the next.

Every so often as we advanced up the hill, Rory ordered a pair of us – one from the day and one from the night-watch – to drop off and hold a position he marked for them. The day-watch member was told to return to his township after that and to return again at first light to relieve his night-watch companion.

'Look-out posts each to supply his own food for the period of duty,' Rory instructed, 'and no communication between posts except by alarm-signal or by messenger from the musket-men.'

I began to realize then how lonely our spells of duty would

be for each of us and I felt sorry for twelve-year-old Elizabeth Ross when she was left standing alone on the hillside. My own post was second from the summit but I did not relish going tamely back home once it had been indicated to me, and so I continued on up the hill along with the men and Lachlan Chisholm who was to be summit look-out for the night-watch.

We stood there for a while surveying the great spread of country below the hill – the moon-rippled waters of the Dornoch Firth to the east, and southwards, the dark gloomy ravine of the Great Pass of Alness cutting through peaks outlined like the ghosts of mountains against the night sky. Neither Rory nor Ian Mackenzie, although they were also on the day-watch, made any move to return down the hill and eventually, by wordless consent, we all moved to squat down in the shelter of a great rock.

There was a feeling of uneasiness in our group that was not entirely accounted for by our purpose on the hill. It came from Rory, from his hand nervously smoothing at the stock of his musket, from his silence and his withdrawn air. I guessed that he was thinking of Jean Chisholm's warning and wondered how long he would keep his own ban of silence about it.

'You should be in your bed if you are to watch tomorrow, Rory,' John Ross said at last.

Rory did not answer him. Instead he turned to me and with a shrug he said, 'These men at least had better be told about Munro, Connal.'

He told them then what Jean Chisholm had said about Munro riding to Tain that night, and it was almost as if they had expected something of this kind for they made little comment when he had finished. Only Lachlan Chisholm, the medical student, pointed downwards and said, 'We will soon know if it is true when we see him riding back up the road,' and Ian Mackenzie said, 'So that is why you are waiting, eh, Rory?'

43

'Aye, I'll not judge anyone but on the evidence of my own eyes,' Rory agreed, and that was all that was said.

We sat in silence, watching the shapes of shadows, hearing the rustle of night-creatures through the grass and heather of the hill-top. It was a companionable silence now that the uneasiness between us was out in the open, and so it did not seem long somehow till the sky began to lighten and the moon paled above us.

In the grey half-light just before dawn, Lachlan Chisholm trained the master's spy-glass on the road. We rose and moved about to take the stiffness from our limbs but kept our eyes on Lachlan so that we knew, by his sudden drawing-in of breath, when he had sighted someone on the road. We closed round him, waiting to hear if he could tell who it was, and soon we could see for ourselves that he was watching a horseman riding up the road towards the hill.

'Munro?' Rory asked.

'I think . . . Yes, it is!' He turned to Rory. 'It *is* Alexander Munro!'

Rory looked at each of us in turn and saw the same doubt and alarm on all our faces. Quietly then, he said:

'Sound the alarm.'

'Sound the alarm?' John Ross repeated doubtfully. 'But he may still be on our side!'

'There is only one way to find that out,' Rory told him grimly. 'Sound the alarm!'

He raised his musket and fired. The other men hesitated, looking questioningly from one to the other, but when Ian Mackenzie raised his musket suddenly and fired it the others followed his example. The last shot was still pealing out as an answering whistle-blast came from farther down the hill. One whistle, then another, and then a constant shrilling of whistles – mine among them as I ran down the hill at the top of my speed.

The hillside was alive with running figures. Girls with their hair flying, skirts kirtled up to their knees, boys leaping like deer over rocks and ditches, waving arms, whistling, shouting. Some I passed, some passed me straining to get back to the boundary before the arrival – as they thought then – of the Sheriff's men, and the farther I ran the more impressed I was with Rory's wisdom in choosing us to stand watch. It was only boys and girls of our age who could have covered the four miles back to the boundary so speedily and still have breath enough to blow the warning as we ran!

We kept to the higher ground, running straight across country and so cutting out the distance that would have been put on our way by the winding of the road in the valley. From this higher ground we had an occasional glimpse of the people streaming out of the townships, and when we came down into the valley at last we saw them standing massed at the boundary. They were waiting silently, shoulder to shoulder, the women clutching the shawls pulled tight over their heads, the men grim and anxious-eyed. A volley of questions greeted our arrival and from behind us Rory's voice called out:

'There is no danger. But stand fast – there may be trouble!'

He strode past me, calling out again: 'Alexander Munro, the tacksman, is on his way back from Tain where he has paid a visit to his law-agent – a visit that suddenly became necessary when he knew we had learned we were in danger of eviction!'

'He will have to answer a few questions, then, before he is allowed back into Greenyards!'

It was my mother, standing in the forefront of the women, who shouted this, and there was an answering shout of angry agreement from the rest of the people. Rory held up a warning hand.

'Quietly, then! He must be near now.'

In the silence that followed his warning we heard faintly the clip-clop of a horse's hooves. The sound grew steadily louder and a few minutes later Munro rounded the bend of the road in front of us and pulled rein in astonishment at the sight that met his eyes.

'What is this? What are you all doing here? What was all that firing and whistling from the hill?'

A silence, each deeper than the last greeted each of his questions, and angrily kicking his horse into motion again he rode right up to where Rory stood in the forefront of the Greenyards people.

'You are behind this unmannerly ploy, Rory Ruadh!'

The accusation was fairly shouted at Rory and his reply was quiet and grave by contrast.

'We find it a strange matter in the present circumstances, Mr. Munro, that you should ride by night to visit your law-agent. That is why we are gathered here. We are afraid for our land, afraid that your visit had something to do with the issue of writs clearing us from the land.'

'I swore to you and that nephew of yours yesterday evening – swore to you before my Maker that I had not put my hand to any such writs!'

His smooth face now red and swollen with rage, Munro leaned out of his saddle towards us and snarled, 'Do any of you doubt such an oath!'

There was a sway and a murmur in the crowd but no one, not even Rory, dared a direct 'yes' to this question.

'You have not denied that your visit to Tain was to see your law-agent,' my mother called suddenly, and another woman's voice took her up with a cry of, 'He cannot deny it, for he knows we would find the truth of it somehow for ourselves!'

There was a buzz of agreement and some laughter at this which seemed to madden Munro. He kicked heels to his horse again, shouting as he urged it forward, 'I'll not stand this prying into my affairs!' but Rory caught his bridle and held the horse in check.

46

'We do not wish to pry,' he told Munro, 'but only to be assured beyond doubt that you will not be a party to putting us out of Greenyards. Give that to us in writing, Mr. Munro, and we will rest content.'

'A gentleman's word is his bond,' Munro snapped, 'and I have given you my word. You will get nothing in writing from me.'

I saw Mr. Aird at this point pushing his way to the front of the crowd, and as Munro finished speaking he cried out:

'Mr. Munro, sir, be patient with them! They may well be in danger of their lives if the writs of eviction are issued and they resist them without this authority from you!'

The people made way for him and he came forward to stand looking up at Munro. The tacksman looked beyond him to where the crowd had closed their ranks again, and in a softened voice he said:

'Of course I understand the position, Mr. Aird. But surely *you* do not doubt my word?'

'You would be taking a terrible sin on your soul to break such a word,' Mr. Aird told him gravely, 'and so I do not doubt you have spoken truly. But it still will not hurt to reassure the doubters among us by putting your promise in writing.'

Munro's hand went up to his face as if he was thinking deeply – or the gesture may have been made to conceal the expression of his features. We could not tell. But when he took his hand away again his face had regained its usual expression of smooth good-humour.

'Very well,' he sighed. 'If it will ease their minds I am prepared to write it out for them.'

'With the oath you swore to me at Braelangwell,' Rory said quickly.

'With any oath you like!'

Now that he had agreed to do it Munro seemed impatient

of all argument and delay, and seeing this, Rory sent one of the boys scudding swiftly across the fields to the nearest house for pen and paper. The tense silence of the crowd broke into chattering and laughing as they waited for his return, but Munro kept a dignified silence that lasted throughout the wait. When the boy returned he wrote the assurance hurriedly on the paper that was handed to him and gave it, still in silence, to Mr. Aird. The minister read it aloud:

'I, Alexander Munro of Braelangwell, do hereby solemnly state and assure the tenants of the farms of Greenyards that, as God is my Maker, I will not sign any writs of eviction that may be issued against them. Given under my hand, this 2nd day of March of the year eighteen hundred and fifty-four.'

There was a loud buzz of approval from the listening people. Munro smiled slightly at the sound and taking the paper back from Mr. Aird he signed it with a quick flourish of his pen. Mr. Aird took it from him again and the murmur from the crowd swelled to a shout as he held it aloft. Munro flicked his mount's reins and drove it forward, his face expressionless now as he bowed stiffly right and left to the crowd making way for him and calling their thanks out as he passed.

Rory took the paper from Mr. Aird and handed it to my mother. 'Keep it safe, Anne,' he advised. 'It will be your best weapon in any argument with the Sheriff or his Officer.'

The other women crowded round her, reaching out their hands to touch the paper as if it were some precious relic, but as soon as she could decently break away from them she thrust it into the pocket of her dress and hurried me away with her. I learned the reason for her haste as soon as we were free of the laughing, chattering groups of people. She stopped, and facing me squarely said:

'Blind John is dead, son. He died about the same time the warning was sounded from the hill.'

I could not prevent the shock of what she said showing in my face for I had loved the old man. She gave me a moment or two to recover myself and then she said:

'The power of speech came back to him before he died and something he said has puzzled me since. He looked at me, Connal, and then he touched my face – oh, so gently, and he said, *"My poor Anne – so they have scarred your face too!"'*

She looked at me curiously. 'You knew him better than most people, Connal. What would make him say such a daft thing to me? My face is not scarred!'

'He was old. His wits would be wandering,' I muttered. But as I spoke I was remembering again the old man's vision of Katrine with blood running down her face, and of someone pointing a pistol at me.

I turned away and as my mother fell in step with me again I hugged myself in a pretence of cold to hide the shiver running over me. The hard outline of the pistol bore painfully into my ribs with the gesture, but I was glad of the feel of it there for under the grief I felt for Blind John there was a feeling of uneasiness about Alexander Munro. It was something to do with the wording of the assurance he had given us – I could not think what, but I had a confused feeling that there was something wrong with it.

5 Drop your pistol, or I will shoot!

Everyone was very satisfied with the working of our alarm system, and with Munro's assurance in our hands, the conviction that Rory's plan was a workable one took firm hold on the people of Greenyards. The boys and girls who were too young to keep watch on the hill with us demanded their share in it also, and were given the task of helping to carry foodstuffs to our secret stores.

In this they played their part with such spirit that it became no uncommon thing to see a group of small children toiling valiantly to carry off a sack of meal as big as one of themselves and scorning a helping hand from anyone older or stronger who happened to pass by. 'The Iron-Ration Brigade', these young ones named themselves, seizing on Rory's description of our stores as the iron rations for the campaign. And even though we older ones teased them about it, they stuck proudly to this name.

The only break in the work of storing food and keeping the watch on Ardgay Hill was for the funeral of Blind John. There was not a single person in the glen who did not follow his coffin to the grave-side, for to have stayed away from his funeral for any reason would, in their eyes, have been a mark of dis-respect to a much-loved and much-respected old man. This was the way of our people and to them anything else would have been less than Christian. Nevertheless, as I looked around me at the crowded grave-side and saw the faces of that day's watch-party among the mourners, I could not help wondering what would have happened if the Sheriff's Officer had chosen that day and time to come to the glen.

As it chanced, however, it was not for another two days that he came, himself and one Witness to the delivery of the writs.

On the morning of that day, the 7th of March, those who were not on watch on the hill said good-bye to Mr. Aird as he set off for Glasgow to visit a journalist on a big newspaper there who was a Ross himself, and whom Mr. Aird was sure would take up our case. We who were on watch saw him riding down the road, and several hours later we saw the approach of the Sheriff-Officer and his Witness.

We gave the warning in good time to gather the people at the boundary of Greenyards and raced down the hill as we had done before. The faces of the Sheriff-Officer and his Witness when they saw us blocking the road into the townships were so comical with dismay that a ripple of laughter ran over the crowd, and it was this laughter that set the tone of our con-versation with them.

The Sheriff-Officer was a big, florid-faced man, William Mac-Pherson by name and known to us in being somewhat slow-witted in situations that called for action. Peter MacKenzie, the constable who was his Witness, was a similar type of man so that, even if they had not been able to size up the situation at a glance, it was no use their putting on blustering airs with us.

For a few minutes only they argued back and forth with us, MacPherson waving the writs he had taken out of his pocket and my mother waving Alexander Munro's assurance under his nose.

'Your writs have no legal force, Mr. MacPherson,' she cried at him, 'for here we have the tacksman's promise that he would not sign them.'

And to his argument that we should examine the writs he carried and see for ourselves that they were in good order, she replied for all of us: 'Indeed we will not, for once these writs are in our hands and the seal on them broken for us to inspect the contents, we shall be held to have taken delivery of them according to the law. And that is what we are determined not to do!'

MacPherson gave up the argument then and put the writs away. 'Well, I have done my duty,' he said with a shrug of his shoulders, 'and the constable here has witnessed that you have resisted me. It will count against you in the end – you must recognize that.'

'We do, but we will not hold you responsible,' Rory told him cheerfully. 'Indeed, we are ready to prove that by giving you our company on the road back as far as Ardgay, and buying you a drink at the inn there to show you that we hold no ill-will against either of you for trying to serve the writs on us.'

Rory's offer was taken up in a burst of laughter by some of the men. They crowded round the Sheriff-Officer and his Witness urging them to take advantage of it, and with another shrug of resignation MacPherson turned his horse and beckoned the constable to do likewise. The men who had urged Rory's offer on them fell in alongside. We others stood for a while watching the small, cheerful cavalcade disappear down the glen before we dispersed to our various duties congratulating ourselves once again on the success that was attending our plan.

The work of building up our secret stores tended to slacken off a bit after this easy rout of the Sheriff-Officer. We gradually grew less and less strict, also, about keeping the positions Rory had allotted us on the hill, for as the days passed and nothing further happened the danger of our situation seemed less urgent. My mother began to worry about Rory having over-stayed his leave from the Army but he quietened her by saying:

'Since my brother cannot be here to stand by his family, Anne, you must allow me to be the best judge of what I do in the circumstances.'

The thought of the punishment that must be building up for him sobered the young people who were on watch, but we were still elated with our first victory and so were not at all put out when, two weeks from the time we had routed MacPherson, another pair of riders into the glen were identified as a Sheriff-Officer and a constable. Once again we sounded the alarm but on this occasion we took our time coming down to the boundary for we anticipated no more trouble with these than we had had with the first two. I was still a good twenty yards from the road, therefore, before I realized how much mistaken we had been.

The bellowing voice of the Sheriff-Officer reached me where I had halted on the steep slope of Cairn Mhor rising up from the roadside, and I slipped my hand inside my jacket to let it rest on my pistol. The man who was shouting was Dugald McCaig, a big black-whiskered fellow with the reputation of having an evil temper and too great a liking for the bottle. He was a dangerous man to cross at any time and now, I realized from the way he was behaving, he was also drunk so that anything was liable to happen within the next few minutes.

The constable who was his Witness was in almost as bad a state as McCaig, roaring and shouting insults at the people who were blocking the way. Rory ran past me and began pushing his way through the mob to try and reach the two officers, but the crowd was too dense to allow him through easily and with every second becoming more and more excited as each one tried and failed to make his voice heard among the shouted arguments.

I stepped slowly down the slope towards the road, my hand still on the pistol and my eyes fixed on McCaig's burly figure swaying in the saddle.

The screaming and shouting that was going on had begun to affect his horse. It reared suddenly, almost throwing him. I had a sudden quick glimpse of my mother, the paper from Munro held aloft in her hand for McCaig to see, throwing up her other arm to protect herself from the plunging hooves. In the same moment McCaig shortened his grasp on the reins, wheeling his horse round to bring it back under control, and as he forced it round to face the crowd again he made a quick grab for the pistol in the holster on his left side.

The hand with the pistol in it shot out at full length from his shoulder. The other hand pulling brutally on the shortened reins held his mount rock-steady while he pressed the muzzle of the pistol against the side of my mother's head. The roaring and surging of the crowd stilled magically into a moment of frozen horror, and into this silence McCaig's voice yelled hoarsely:

'I'll show you how to deal with rebellious scum like this woman!'

I was twenty feet away from him by this time, to one side of him and out of the range of his forward vision. No one in the crowd facing him dared move or speak as he spun out the suspense of the moment it took to draw back his trigger-finger. My mother stood like a stone woman, only the wide terror of her eyes showing that she knew her life hung on whichever way the balance of McCaig's drunken rage would swing.

All this passed through my mind with a coolness of deliberation that astonished me, so that although it took only the same flash of time for me to draw my own pistol, it seemed to me that I had done so calmly and without haste. I covered McCaig and shouted:

'Drop your pistol, McCaig, or stand the consequences!'

McCaig's arm remained steadily extended as my voice rang out but the hand holding his pistol wavered slightly. Slowly he turned his head till his eyes could take me in. I kept my pistol pointing towards him and met his glare calmly. His eyes flickered down to my right hand. I guessed he was trying to make up his mind whether the pistol I held was loaded and if so whether I would keep my nerve enough to shoot.

'Drop your pistol,' I called again, 'or I will shoot *now*!'

McCaig's pistol hand dropped slowly to his side. My mother sagged suddenly down, was caught and held by Katrine and John Ross between them. Above the threatening murmur that broke from the crowd as she fell, McCaig broke into loud and unconvincing laughter, thrusting his pistol back into its holster and shouting, 'Ah, you are ninnies, all of you! It was only for a joke I drew on the woman!'

His last words were almost lost in the shout that swelled out of the crowd's murmur. A voice screaming 'Seize them!' rose above the shout. Other voices took up the cry and added to it.

'Strip them! Tear the warrants up!'

I stayed silent and kept my pistol levelled. The constable had made no move to follow McCaig's example when he drew on my mother and he had not attempted to intervene when I threatened to shoot. His hand was now suspiciously near his pistol holster, however, and so I stayed still and silent where I was.

The crowd began to mill round the two men, hemming them in from retreat back down the glen and forcing their horses close together. Hands reached up to them, plucking and tearing at any hold they could get on their uniforms. They fought the hands off, striking down at heads and kicking out with booted feet, but first one man and then another caught a foot that lashed out at him and both McCaig and the constable were tumbled out of their saddles.

The crowd pounced on them joyously then, jerking them

upright while hands went rapidly through their pockets, seizing the warrants and waving them triumphantly aloft before they were torn to shreds and scattered broadcast on the dark, rapid flow of the Carron's waters. McCaig and the constable stood hang-dog and sullen as the pieces of paper fluttered through the air and sank down on the water, and seeing his downcast air the people could not forbear to tease McCaig with his own words.

'Will you not laugh then, Mr. McCaig, at the great joke *we* are having?' Rory invited him, and tore the stiff paper of a writ across with a rending noise right under McCaig's nose.

'Och aye, Rory, he is the great man for joking! He will surely laugh at this!' Peter Ross protested, mock-solemn. And with laughter coming from all sides now, the jeering went on.

'He came to the glen for a joke and he is getting plenty to laugh at now!'

'Will you be needing a pistol at you again to make you laugh, McCaig?'

'Look at Mistress Ross there! She has nearly died laughing at his joke with the pistol!'

My mother was very far indeed from laughing. She was leaning against a great boulder at the side of the road, her face as white as her kerchief. Katrine was bathing her brow with water she had dipped from the river and old Kirsty Ross, a neighbour of ours, was anxiously chafing her hands. I took one more glance at the crowd on the road before I went down to her.

They were lifting McCaig and the constable bodily back on to their horses, still loudly jeering at them for the 'joke' that had misfired. McCaig's eyes met mine. His face twisted into a snarl and he screamed at me:

'You will pay for this, you young dog! I'll hunt you down and crush you! I'll see you strung up —'

I turned away stopping my ears against the curses streaming from him, but behind my back as I went down to my mother I heard his voice raving still above the shouts and laughter that sent the two men on their way again. I slid my pistol back into my belt thinking to myself how different the outcome might have been if I had not been able to threaten McCaig with it, and it was only then that I remembered Blind John's saying in his vision:

'Watch out for his pistol, Connal! He is going to shoot!'

I stopped dead in my tracks as it struck me that it must have been this incident that the old man had foreseen. My mother's voice brought me back to my surroundings again.

'Where did you get it, Connal?' she was demanding. 'How did *you* manage to get hold of a pistol?'

'It was the one in the thatch,' I told her. 'The one grandfather showed me long ago.'

'Is it loaded?'

I nodded and she cried out in horror. 'Oh, dear God! Where would we have been if the young fool had killed McCaig! Give it to me this instant, boy! Give it here!'

I looked from her face to Katrine's and from Katrine's face to those of the women who had gathered around her, and last of all I looked at Rory standing gravely listening behind her. My mother was all angry determination. The women's faces were tense and curious, but Rory's face was blank of any expression. None of them was of any help to me as my mother advanced with her hand imperiously outstretched to take the pistol. I held my ground in front of her, clutching the pistol to me with one hand and warding off her advance with the other.

'Where would *you* have been,' I asked rapidly, 'if I had not been able to draw on McCaig?'

She halted, staring at me, with the blood rising like a red stain against the whiteness of her cheeks. Her eyes searched my face as if she had never seen me before in her life and was wondering who on earth I was and then in a small voice she said, 'Connal . . . oh, Connal!' and collapsed against me, weeping as if her heart would break.

Rory took her gently from me and held her. 'There, there, lassie. Cry away,' he said soothingly. His eyes met mine over her head.

'I intend to keep the pistol,' I told him.

Rory nodded. 'It is your decision to make. You are the one most likely to be in danger from McCaig now.'

The women gathered round then and led my mother away towards our house. We followed them slowly, not speaking to one another till Rory said, 'It is counted a serious offence to threaten an officer of the law with a fire-arm. We must be ready for the worst now.'

He stopped and waited till the rest of the men had gathered round us and then, raising his voice so that they could all hear, he said:

'McCaig has threatened to be revenged on Connal for this, even though he brought the whole matter on himself. But he can only move against him through all of you. You must pass the word, therefore, to stand by for their coming back in great numbers now, and pray – all of you – that Mr. Aird has some success before that happens.'

We went slowly back to the townships, each group chattering of what had happened and of what still had to be done if we were to succeed in holding off any attempt to get us out of the glen by force. No one spoke of my drawing the pistol, either to praise or blame me for it. I was not surprised at this for I could see as clearly as any of them that, although I had had no choice but to act as I did, the incident might well prove a turning point in the Sheriff's decisions about us.

'How long will it be now before we can expect to hear from Mr. Aird?' I asked Rory, and confidently he answered:

'It should be soon. It is two weeks, after all, since he left the glen, and that is time enough for him to have reached Glasgow and to have arranged matters there with his journalist friend. We are almost certain to hear from him before another week has passed.'

'A week is not long,' I said, relieved. 'We can surely hold out till then.'

'Indeed we can,' Rory agreed. 'And even if we do have to flee to the higher reaches, a few days in the open – a few weeks even – will not hurt us.'

'They will burn our houses if we run away as you say we must.'

Katrine had lagged behind the group of women round my mother and now she had joined us in time to take part in the conversation. Rory looked down at her with a grim little smile.

'So they will, Katrine. So they will. But houses can be re-built. Once we leave the glen, however, we will never be allowed to return.'

'And so long as we can stay,' I finished for him, 'the glen will be ours.'

Katrine smiled at me, and in a sudden sense of comradeship with her that lifted my spirits, I smiled back at her. She drew closer to me and whispered curiously, 'Connal, why did you take the pistol from the thatch in the first place?'

'To protect *you*, of course,' I said with what I hoped she would take for mock-gallantry, and was thankful when she greeted this with laughter that showed she had no idea how truly I had answered.

One part of Blind John's vision had come true, after all, and so I was more than ever determined not to let her guess anything of the other danger he had foreseen – the danger that threatened herself.

6 We have broken the law

From the day that I pulled the pistol on Sheriff-Officer Mc-Caig, we were like a people in a state of siege.

None dared absent himself from the glen for fear he might be missing when the testing moment came. The piling-up of our stores was completed. The cattle were penned, ready for the men to drive off. Our own few sheep were driven up to just below the snow-line on the Bodach Mhor, the great mountain escarpment that sheltered the glen's western reaches, there to survive as best they might.

It was with heavy hearts that we turned them loose on the mountainside, for these soft-woolled sheep of ours were nothing like the heavy, coarse-fleeced animals the Lowlanders had brought north in such droves. They were small beside the Lowland breed, delicate in comparison to their hardy strain. Each one of them had been named by us at birth and tended afterwards with care and gentleness, and the affection we felt for them was only equalled by our hatred of the alien breed that was eating up all the little farms of the Highland glens. Still, the cattle had to come first for it was the cattle that gave us our livelihood and not the sheep.

The only news we had of outside events during this time was from a tribe of tinkers passing through the glen on their way to the west, and from them we learned that the towns of Tain and Inverness were both in a great stir over what had happened, Sheriff-Officer McCaig having told a terrible tale of riot and deforcement in his report. It was 'the Greenyards rioters' they were calling us now in the towns, and the land-owning gentry, fearful of such behaviour spreading to the few down-trodden tenants who had survived the clearances on their own lands, were pressing Sheriff Taylor to enforce the writs of eviction against us. The Sheriff himself, said the travelling people, was mad as a turkey-cock with rage at his men being twice turned back.

We thanked the tinkers and gave them of our charity for even such bleak news, and kept the watch more strictly than we had ever done.

On the 31st of March, then, nine days from the time McCaig had been sent running from the glen, I found myself beside Lachlan Chisholm just after our watch had marched at dawn to relieve the night-watch. Still no mes-senger had arrived from Mr. Aird. I was thinking of this as Lachlan stopped beside me on his way down from the summit of the hill, and wondering just what Mr. Aird hoped to accomplish through his friendship with the journalist, Donald Ross.

'Is he a good writer, then, this Donald Ross?' I asked Lachlan, thinking he might have read some of the man's work while he was studying at the University. Lachlan considered my question.

'Some say he is, but there are others who say that he lets his pen run away with him.'

'But he *is* well known?'

'Oh, aye, indeed – for the fiery nature of him, if for nothing else! He is a great one for taking up causes.'

'And would you say that people will heed him if he writes our story in the newspapers?'

'It is not so much that we have to worry about, Connal, as whether he can get a hearing for us at all!'

'Why should he not?' I demanded. 'Surely such a thing is worth putting in a newspaper?'

'It depends on what else is happening at the time,' Lachlan explained patiently. 'For instance, just before I left Glasgow there was a lot of talk about a war happening between England and Russia. Now, if such an event *did* happen, the newspapers would be so full of it they would have no room for any news about us. People would not be interested in us anyway, with such a big matter to worry them!'

He went on down the hill leaving me wondering if this war he spoke of had started and if that was why we had not heard from Mr. Aird. It seemed curious to me that something which might have happened thousands of miles away could affect our fortunes, and I continued in thought about it for some time after Lachlan had gone.

It was still barely light at this time and the night-watch going home were only shadowy figures vanishing down the glen. It was cold, with a frosty little wind that set me walking about and stamping my feet to warm them. The prospect of another day's uneventful watch on the hill depressed me. As the light strengthened I thought longingly of the warm bed I had left, and stopped my stamping to crouch down out of the wind's path in the lee of a rock jutting from the hillside.

I had hardly settled into position when the sound of a musket-shot brought me leaping to my feet again. I fumbled for my whistle but before it reached my lips another shot shattered the air, and then another. I blew a shrill, continuous blast, waving with my free arm to those below and above me on the hill. Then I set off running, keeping up as many blasts on the whistle as my breath would allow. Still the musket-shots continued, but it was not till I had been running and blowing for several hundred yards that I realized this properly and remembered what it meant. The Sheriff had come in force against us!

I stopped and turned to stare up the hill. Rory and Ian Mackenzie were outlined against the summit, the raised muskets projecting from their shoulders looking like two thin black sticks against the pale light of the sky. The black sticks puffed out smoke again. The crack of the shots that followed released my feet – my tongue as well, for as I turned to run again I let out such a bellow of excitement as nearly burst my lungs.

I ran as I never had in my life before. I overtook the twins, Donald and Ewan Munro, and the three of us pounding on were joined farther down the hill by a girl called Naomi Ross running as fleet as a deer from a point to the left of us. We exchanged looks, but no words passed between us. All our breath was saved for running and blowing on our whistles. The shooting behind us continued steadily, and from the point where we could glimpse the far-off townships, we saw a furious activity of men and cattle.

The length of time they had to get clear away depended on the point at which the Sheriff's forces had been sighted, and remembering that the visibility had been reasonably good at the time the first shots were fired I prayed this meant they would have the hour that Rory had estimated on the night of the schoolhouse meeting.

We neared the slope of Cairn Mhor rising up from the roadside at the meeting-place and Ewan Munro pointed to it, gasping:

'We will have the best view of what is happening from there!'

'No, the road is the best place to watch from,' his twin, Donald, flung back at him. 'I am going down beside the crowd.'

The opinion was split like this for all of us when we actually reached the boundary. Some of the boys and girls plunged straight on to join the crowd of women drawn up in their silent ranks across the road. Others, myself among them, flung ourselves down on the slope of the hill and prepared to watch events from there.

It was a good vantage point. From it I could distinguish my mother standing in the front rank of the women, and I could also see my grandfather's white head towering above the mass of their red-shawled heads. John Ross and his brother Peter were there also with Lachlan Chisholm, almost as tall as they were, beside them. I could see nothing of Katrine, however, although I knew she must be somewhere in the crowd, and so I turned from the road to look back up the hill at the figures of Ian Mackenzie and Rory growing steadily larger as they too made for the meeting-place.

There was utter silence among the women and the only sounds now that the whistling and firing had stopped were the running footsteps of those still making for the boundary and the occasional shout that passed between them. Thus matters continued for another ten to fifteen minutes and then we heard the faint sound of hoof-beats from the Sheriff's troop. Those of us on the hillside rose slowly to our feet, straining our ears towards the sound. Rory and Ian were almost up on us now, and by the time the hoof-beats had grown to a steady clattering of iron on stone, Rory was standing panting by my side.

'How many are there of them?' I demanded.

Rory gave a quick glance towards the now-deserted townships. 'About forty I would say, not counting whoever is in the two carriages they have with them.'

They rounded the corner a few moments later. At the signal of the officer riding at their head, the men dismounted and formed up in ranks on the road. I caught sight of Dugald Mc-Caig in a group of Sheriff-Officers at the rear of the ranks of constables and a little twinge of fear went through me. Instinctively I moved closer to Rory Ruadh and as I did so the door of each carriage opened. Sheriff Taylor himself dismounted from one and from the other came two men one of whom Rory identified for me as Donald Stewart, the law-agent to Alexander Munro, and the other as the law-officer known as the Procurator Fiscal.

These two stayed where they were but Sheriff Taylor came to the head of the ranks of constables and shouted to the women, first in English and then in Gaelic, telling them to disperse. None of them moved and in the tension of the moment following on the Sheriff's shout I caught hold of Rory's sleeve, digging my fingers into his arm.

'Easy, now, easy,' he whispered reprovingly. 'They are doing nothing against the law and so they are in no danger.'

I took my hand away again, raging inwardly at the necessity of meeting the Sheriff thus with passive resistance when every instinct of my fighting Highland heritage urged me towards open battle with his men.

As the women stayed silent and unmoving, the Sheriff pulled a paper from his pocket and began to read aloud from it. It was the Riot Act he was reading. I recognized the wording from what I had learned at school, but the Sheriff was speaking in English now and what he said made no sense to many of the women. Some of them began shouting above the sound of his voice, calling out that they had an assurance from the tacksman that made any writs against us invalid. My mother held it up in her hand for the Sheriff to see and the ranks of women behind her began to sway as they tried to press forward towards him.

Rory gave a quick, uneasy glance at the slope behind us and on the women's right, another one at the dark roll of the Carron's waters on the women's left. I could see it passing through his mind that the Sheriff would not be reading the Riot

Act unless he meant his men to push forward immediately, and that if they did so, some of the women might be injured by the resulting crush in the narrow defile between Cairn Mhor and the River Carron.

The Sheriff finished his reading. He made a great show of folding the paper and returning it to his pocket, and on the gesture Rory shouted:

'Hold your hand, Sheriff!'

And to the women he shouted, 'Clear the way there! Do you hear me? Things have gone too far for talk now! Get quickly away to join the children and the men-folk now, all of you!'

The parade-ground roar of his voice rose above the cries of the women. Some of them heeded him immediately and backed out of the crowd. Some of them ignored him by pressing forward more determinedly than ever, and others re-doubled their cries for the Sheriff to read Alexander Munro's assurance.

'Clear the way!' the Sheriff shouted in his turn, but a woman standing beside my mother snatched the paper from her hand and sprang forward with it, waving it right under his nose.

'It is *our* way!' she cried passionately. 'See, here we have the right to it written down for us!'

The Sheriff's head jerked back from the waving paper. With a sweep of his arm he sent the woman flying to one side, and in a voice high with rage he screamed:

'*Knock them down!*'

The constables drew their batons and charged. For a split second I was aware only of the mass of uniformed men with their forest of upraised batons bearing down on the women, then the roar of anguished disbelief from Rory at my side broke the spell that held me rigid. As the front rank of women broke and went down under the swinging batons I leaped down the slope and plunged into the nightmare heart of the attack.

I had to reach my mother on the far side of it and somehow I had to find Katrine – both impossible tasks. I was wedged, pushed, sent stumbling and sprawling as the dense mass of women struggled vainly to retreat from the place which, from being so easy to block, had turned even more easily into a deadly trap. My ears were filled with the sound of screaming, with the savage shouts of the constables, and with cries and groans of pain from those already wounded.

I could see what was happening only in snatches. I saw Naomi Ross, the girl who had sped side by side with me down the hill, run screaming from the upraised batons of a Sheriff-Officer and two constables. The river blocked her path. She plunged into it and surfaced waist-deep a few feet from the bank. The Sheriff-Officer turned to beckon the two constables to follow him and I saw it was Dugald McCaig leading the pursuit. He splashed into the river after Naomi. The constables followed him and all three struck savagely at Naomi's head. She sank beneath the blows and surfaced again to clutch despairingly at McCaig. His baton crunched down again on her head in a blow that sent her finally under the water.

Seconds later I saw an older woman wrest the baton from the hand of one of the girl's attackers, and then herself suffer the same fate.

Ewan Munro went down under a baton-stroke to the head. Donald Munro dropped to his knees beside the body of his twin, crying out in grief and rage over it. The man who had felled Ewan yelled, 'I'll keep you from crying!' and his baton smashed down on Donald's skull in its turn.

I stumbled across the body of my grandfather, his white head lying in a pool of blood. I saw Rory catch up a constable round the waist, raise him high in the air, whirl him bodily round his head and then throw him with a great splash into the River Carron.

I saw twelve-year-old Elizabeth Ross retreating in terror among the women who tried to scramble away from the batons up the side of Cairn Mhor; saw her beaten to her knees by a rain of baton-blows, and her older sisters Janet and Margaret running to help her, savagely attacked in their turn.

Then I saw Rory again, four constables round him and himself backing towards the river in a losing battle that finished with him being toppled into the water, striking his head against a rock as he fell and disappearing beneath the swift flow of the current.

And all the time these things were happening I was twisting and feinting away from batons myself, landing a punch or a kick at the constables where the chance offered, shouldering aside when I could the charge of a constable at the terrified women milling round me. I was more than half-dazed by glancing blows within a few minutes of plunging downhill, and I had given up all hope of finding my mother and sister when I heard Katrine's voice screaming:

'Connal! Help me! *Help me!*'

I whirled in the direction of her scream and saw her crouched a few feet from me with both hands trying to shield her head from a baton swinging down at her. Her hair was wild, her face was the face of Blind John's vision – streaked scarlet with the blood that trickled down it. I threw myself sideways, landing bodily on her to bear her backwards out of the danger-line, and as we toppled the blow intended for her crashed down on my left shoulder. I heard the crunch and felt the agony of breaking bone before a second blow descended on my head and blotted out everything for me.

It was Katrine's voice once again that brought me back to consciousness, Katrine weeping and imploring me:

'Wake up, Connal, wake up! Margaret is dead and they have taken mother off to the gaol. Wake up, *please*, Connal!'

I opened my eyes. The sky swung dizzily above me. I felt Katrine's hands on either side of my face and realized I was lying with my head in her lap. I turned my head sideways with an effort that sent daggers of pain shooting through my skull.

There was a face on the grass beside me, the face of Katrine's friend, Margaret Munro. The front of her head was a mess of blood and shattered bone. Her long hair, soaked in blood, lay in twisted strands across the gaping wound. I jerked my head away from the sight, and rolling off Katrine's knees fell face downwards, groaning, against the grass.

It was wet against my face, wet not with dew or rain, but with blood. I pushed myself away from it, raising myself upwards on my one good hand and longing to lose consciousness again, but I could not. Katrine was at my side, plucking at me, dragging me to my feet. I cast my right arm round her neck and we stood swaying together, holding on to one another.

'You are hurt,' I said foolishly.

My tongue felt thick in my mouth and I could hardly get the words out. I peered at the long, ugly wound pouring blood from her scalp and tried to bring my left hand up to touch it, but my arm would not lift from my side. I remembered the blow on my shoulder then – I remembered everything, and I turned my head from Katrine to stare slowly around at the scene of the attack.

Bodies lay everywhere, on the road, the river-bank, the side of the hill – some prone where they had fallen, some crouched, some struggling feebly to rise. And blood was scattered everywhere, on the grass, the stones, the clothes of the stricken figures. It was like the scene of a battle-field, I thought, except that this had not been a battle but a massacre. And I tried to feel anger, but all I could feel was the pain in my head and shoulder and a terrible, heart-rending grief for our foolish optimism in believing that even the Sheriff's men would never sink so low as to attack our women.

I sank down on the grass again, and deprived of our mutual support, Katrine collapsed to her knees beside me.

'Is Grandfather alive?' I whispered, and she said dully, 'Only just.'

'And Rory?'

'He is gone – swept away by the river.'

I had no strength to speak or move again, and neither had Katrine. We crouched there for I cannot tell how long, with the cries of pain from the wounded sounding horribly in our ears. I think I fell into a sort of stupor, for it was only very gradually I became aware of other voices. It was Lachlan Chisholm I heard first and I was vaguely aware it must be him only because of the way he spoke.

'Margaret Munro, frontal and parietal bones shattered,' he was saying, and raising my head slowly I saw him bending down to examine the body of Katrine's friend. There were other figures beyond him, those of the men who had driven off the stock, and the sounds I could hear now were their cries of grief and rage as they moved among the wounded.

Lachlan rose to his feet and I saw Peter Ross kneeling on the far side of Margaret Munro's body. Peter's head was bleeding and his left arm hung crookedly at his side, but he rose vigorously enough to his feet as Lachlan said:

'The wounded must be housed under the one roof if I am to attend them all. Try and gather the men together, Peter, and have those unable to walk carried down to the schoolhouse. And someone must ride to Tain for a doctor – two doctors if possible.'

Peter did not move. He looked down at Margaret Munro, and with anguish twisting his features he said,

'Heaven will never forgive us leaving our women-folk to be massacred like this!'

'That is foolish talk,' Lachlan told him sharply, 'and I, for one, will not listen to it. No one could have foreseen a vicious attack like this, man! The worst that any reasonable person could have expected was that the women would be shouldered aside – not beaten as savagely as if they had been mad wolves! And you heard what old Donald Ban said, after all, when we

70

spoke to him back there. Nine campaigns he has fought in nine different countries, and never has he seen such savagery turned against helpless women-folk.'

Peter rose slowly to his feet and walked away. Lachlan stood looking after him for a moment then he bent down and picked up a folded sheet of paper lying beside Margaret Munro. It was stiff paper that crackled as he smoothed out the folds. I rose to my knees and slowly forced myself to stand upright and take the step that enabled me to look over his shoulder.

The paper was a writ of eviction. Through the blood that smeared it I could distinguish the legal phrasing of the words, and at the foot of it I saw the bold flowing signature of Alexander Munro of Braelangwell. Lachlan pointed to the signature and said indigantly:

'And him swearing before his Maker that he would not be a party to putting us out! So much for promises!'

I realized then what had worried me about the wording of Munro's assurance to us, and with rage and bitterness nearly choking me I said:

'He has not broken any promise – oh, no! Not *that* cunning one! Do you not see, Lachlan? The writs were *already signed* when he made it.'

I pointed to the date – the 1st of March, at the head of the paper. 'That was the date of the schoolhouse meeting – the date of the night he rode to see his law-agent. The writs must have been ready for him – he must have signed them then. And it was on the morning of the following day – the 2nd of March, that he gave us an assurance that he would not sign any writs *that might be issued against us*. But that promise meant nothing at all, for the wording of it referred only to something that might happen in the future. It had nothing to do with the writs already signed!'

Lachlan's eyes followed my pointing finger. 'So the law was on the Sheriff's side after all when he ordered his men to attack!' He crumpled the writ up and let it drop from his fingers. 'There were more of these writs lying scattered among the wounded,' he said quietly. He sighed and stood looking around at the prone bodies and the grief-stricken men that moved among them. 'It is a high price we have paid for trying to hold our land.'

'There will be higher yet to pay,' I told him, 'now that we have broken the law – the noble law that says we must not resist when Englishmen and Lowlanders try to wrest the five hundred years of our inheritance from us and give it to sheep to eat! We have still to pay for *that* "crime".'

7 *You must get away quickly!*

I did not go to the schoolhouse to be treated along with the rest of the wounded for I could see that Lachlan would have his hands more than full with those who were seriously injured. I went instead with Katrine to look for my grandfather and between us we managed to get the old man home.

His head had been cut, and though he had no bones broken he was stunned and badly bruised, and the shock to his system had left only a feeble flicker of life in him. We made him warm and comfortable and then we attended to one another's hurts as best we could. As I bandaged her head with my one good hand, Katrine told me how the constables had seized our mother and three other women, chained them, and dragged them off down the glen.

'How badly was she hurt?' I asked, and sobbing, Katrine told me that one side of her face had been laid open to the bone by a baton-blow.

I had picked up one of these batons as we left the scene of the attack. It was made of ash wood, as hard and nearly as heavy as iron, and bound with strips of copper. The monogram V.R., Victoria Regina, had been worked in copper also on the handle – Victoria Regina, a mother of children, a woman of about my own mother's age, a plump woman with soft-skinned cheeks like hers! It must have been the edge of one of her metalled monograms that had torn *my* mother's cheek to the bone, I thought, and seeing the horrified look I turned on the baton as she spoke Katrine added through her sobs:

'The others are even worse, Connal. Old Kirsty Ross was so badly wounded that she might not reach Tain alive!'

'We must *do* something!' I said wildly. 'We cannot just sit here and let them die!'

My grandfather's eyes opened at this. 'The Sheriff will not let them die,' he said in a feeble voice. 'He cannot bring four corpses to trial.'

I stared at him, thinking I would go mad in another moment with the horror of it all, but Katrine said in her normal voice:

'That is perfectly true, Connal. They are bound to get a doctor to them in gaol. What we have to do now is to find out what everyone else intends – and we must find Rory Ruadh.'

I had forgotten that the last I had seen of Rory was his disappearing under the water of the River Carron. Katrine's words reminded me and gave me something to do that satisfied my restless urge for action. I left her then, in charge of my grandfather, and went searching for Rory.

There was a chance that he might have been swept ashore at the ford a quarter of a mile east of Greenyards. It was towards this that I hurried at the best pace I could and, as I had hoped, I found him there. I was not a moment too soon, however, for he was lying half-in and half-out of the water and so near-drowned that he was slipping farther and farther back into it with every second that passed.

There was a huge lump on one temple where his head had struck the rock before he went down, but he was conscious enough to know me when I spoke to him. I gave him my right hand to grasp and set my teeth against the long, slow agony of helping him to drag himself out on to the riverbank.

I collapsed beside him once he was out of the water, my injured shoulder on fire with pain and my head spinning wildly with the effort I had made. Rory's voice came back to him as we lay helpless there together, and he babbled weakly in self-reproach for the way his plan had resulted in the women being trapped in the narrow pass between Cairn Mhor and the river. I heard him only vaguely through the daze of my own pain and weakness, and it was a long time before the two of us managed to begin the nightmare effort of helping one another up and staggering back towards home.

Katrine had hot soup ready for us and blankets to wrap ourselves in when we had stripped off our sodden clothes. She had also been down to the schoolhouse, and as we slowly spooned up our soup she told us of the situation there.

Of the women and the girls injured by the batons, she said, eighteen had broken bones or fractured skulls. These were all in a serious condition, and although Margaret Munro whom we had taken for dead was still miraculously clinging to a tiny thread of life, one other woman had since died of her injuries and another had gone mad.

Peter Ross had organized the stretcher parties which brought the wounded to the schoolhouse. He had also sent a messenger posting to Tain to find out what had happened to the women who had been arrested and another messenger to call both the doctors who practised in Tain to come urgently to Greenyards. Lachlan Chisholm, meanwhile, had turned the schoolhouse into a makeshift infirmary and was doing what he could to ease the pain of those who had been brought there.

I thought of the time, two years ago, when every family in the glen had gladly given their little contribution towards the payment of Lachlan's University fees. Proud, they had been, that one of us should be called to the noble profession of medicine, and thinking of this I said bitterly, 'I'll wager there is not one of them dreamt that Lachlan would ever be called on to repay them in *this* kind!'

No one said anything. I looked at them one by one – Katrine, Rory Ruadh, my grandfather. Their faces were blank, their eyes blind as each one stared in horror at an inner vision of the savagery that had been turned against us. I thought then that they looked like people who had died and seen hell.

'What happened to the paper with Munro's assurance on it?' I asked at last. Not that I thought it was any use to us now, but if the Sheriff intended to bring my mother and the other three women to trial it would at least prove they had acted in good faith.

'Lost – or stolen. We do not know which,' Katrine said wearily. 'The men searched all the ground at the boundary, but there was no sign of it.'

She turned to Rory. 'And that is only the beginning of our troubles now. They will come for *you* soon, Rory Ruadh. Your leave is weeks overstayed already.'

'Why should I care what happens to me?' he said despairingly. 'My name is Ishmael among my people now, for I am the cause of their sorrow.'

From this attitude, nothing would move him. He was a changed man, Rory Ruadh, after that day. The warm, genial nature of him froze into a bitter, quiet coldness, and he made no further reference to what had happened except on the third day after the attack when he rode into Tain to engage a lawyer to defend my mother at her trial. He told us what he had done and that the lawyer's fee had been paid. Then he gave Katrine the rest of the money he had drawn from the bank in Tain for that purpose. She knew – we both knew very well that this was the Army pay he had been saving against the day he would retire from active service and come back to live in the glen, and

76

Katrine would not take it from him. He seized her hand and bundled the money into it.

'Take it! You will get little enough from the sale of the stock and the money is no use to me,' he said roughly. 'There will be no glen to come back to when *I* retire.'

Two days after that, the military patrol we had all expected to come some time for him appeared to take him into custody, and he went with them without protest.

I heard the gruff rumble of the patrol's voices from the inner room where I lay at the time, for I had shot my bolt with the effort of dragging Rory from the water and since then the pain of my broken shoulder together with the drenching I had suffered had thrown me into a fever. The voices rose and fell in my dulled hearing, and then Rory came through to the inner room and began to change back into his uniform.

'They have come from Fort George to fetch me,' he said, seeing my eyes turned on him. 'The regiment has been ordered south.'

'Will they be hard on you?' I asked.

'Hard enough,' he said indifferently. 'I will not get off under five hundred lashes at the least.'

I turned my face away, sickened by the thought. Rory came over to me when he had finished dressing and turned my face towards him again.

'It was *not* your fault,' I said before he could speak. 'They came like savage beasts, not like men! You could not be expected to think they would act like beasts!'

He brushed this aside and said urgently, 'Listen well, Connal, for soon I will be in a far country and not able to help you, even with advice.'

I clutched at him. 'Where? Where are they sending you, Rory?'

'To Russia,' he told me, 'to some place called the Crimea. It seems that war has broken out between England and Russia and my regiment is ordered to the front line.'

His words were like a blow on the face to me. This was the threatened war that Lachlan had spoken of – the tragic great event that would destroy all our hopes of making a stir in the newspapers with the story of our little sorrows. I loosed my hold on Rory and sank back on the pillow, so choked with disappointment that I could not speak.

'Are you heeding my words?' Rory asked. I nodded dumbly, and he went on, 'Well, then, this Hector Cameron – the lawyer I have engaged to defend your mother has been well paid to fight her case and he is a very shrewd man. He will defend her well and, moreover, he knows all about McCaig's threats to be revenged on you for drawing the pistol on him. Take his advice in anything that happens in either of these matters and you will not go far wrong. You understand?'

I nodded again and he took my hand in a firm clasp. 'Then God be with you all now for I cannot linger here another moment. If I do, and it wartime, they will drag me off to be shot as a deserter.'

Bending over me he laid his hand lightly for a moment on the brow of my grandfather breathing feebly beside me, and then he was gone. I lay still for a minute or two and then, when I heard the footsteps of the patrol departing, I tumbled out of bed and went unsteadily to the window.

Katrine found me crouched there watching the bright splash of scarlet from their tunics disappearing down the glen, and tried to drive me back into bed. I ignored her scolding and fumbled for my clothes for I was determined now to get back on my feet and play an active part again in the resistance to the Sheriff.

I told Katrine so but she said sadly: 'There is no more talk of resistance, Connal. Everyone is too shocked by what has taken place. They are like people who have been stunned and cannot think properly. Besides, the writs have been served and they are legal. What can we do but wait for them to evict us?'

I sat on the edge of the bed looking at her and trying to

realize that there was no answer to this – that only someone in my fevered state would need to be told how hopeless our position had become. Yet still some urge drove me to continue dressing so that I had at least the appearance of activity. And seeing how set I was on this Katrine gave in to me and helped me through to sit by the fire while she continued her work about the house.

So we passed another two days, with me dozing and useless by the fire but gradually gaining strength again, and with Katrine continuing to cook and clean as well as looking after me and our grandfather. She even found time to go out daily to help with the nursing in the schoolhouse, and watching her I marvelled at the way she had kept her feet despite the severity of her own wound.

People came and went in our house during this time. One of the doctors from Tain looked in and pronounced my broken shoulder set and beginning to heal, and both Peter Ross and Lachlan Chisholm came and talked to me. I answered them only briefly for I was too sunk in my own thoughts to trouble with conversation. I kept remembering my mother touching her cheek and saying wonderingly, *'My face is not scarred'*, and trying to put from my mind the dreadful wound that must be there now. And I kept thinking how all of Blind John's visions had come true and wondering in a dull sort of way what worse could possibly happen to us. Lachlan and Peter got little sense out of me and when they turned from me to talk to Katrine I ignored the conversation altogether.

I would have been better prepared for the next crisis that came upon us if I had not been so wrapped in my own thoughts, but as it was I was taken completely by surprise when Katrine came home from the schoolhouse one day a week after the Sheriff's attack. Lachlan and Peter followed close on her heels as she came through the door. Peter closed the door behind them and Katrine said quietly to me :

'Connal, the Messenger-at-Arms from the Sheriff's office in Tain has come to search for the one that pulled the pistol on Dugald McCaig. All the boys in the townships are to be brought out for questioning and the houses searched. You must get away quickly – as quickly as you can.'

I heard without understanding properly at first. 'Where?' I asked stupidly. 'Where can I go?'

Lachlan reached for my jacket and came towards me with it. 'The cave on the Bodach Mhor,' he said briskly. 'Hurry, Connal, they will be starting the search presently.'

The meaning of Katrine's words had penetrated properly by this time and crying out 'No!' I backed away from Lachlan.

'They have arrested my mother. If she can take her chance with them, then I must too. Let them arrest me as well!'

'Young fool!' Peter Ross caught my arm and hustled it into my jacket sleeve. '*You* threatened to shoot an officer of the law! Do you realize the charge they could make out of that action in the circumstances we are in now? Get on with you, if you do not want to rot in gaol for the best years of your life!'

He turned to Katrine. 'Have you the food and blankets ready for him?'

Katrine nodded and pointed to a bundle lying in a corner by the door. Lachlan took hold of it and swung it on his back and I realized that they must have been expecting something like this and preparing for it all the time I was ill. I went unresisting to the door with them. Katrine followed us and at the door she said to Peter:

'You have quite made up your mind to go through with the bargain, Peter?'

I tried to push Lachlan's hands away from me and turn round. 'What bargain? What is Peter —'

'Connal, there is no time to explain. You must hurry,' Lachlan interrupted, pulling me through the door with him. And before I knew where I was he had me out of the house and standing at the front door. From there we could see down to the schoolhouse where a number of boys of my own age were already lined up in front of a small knot of uniformed men.

'If we keep to the bed of the river they will not see us going up the glen,' Lachlan said.

'See *us*? Are you coming with me?'

'You would not manage half a mile of the journey by yourself, let alone the climb up the side of the Bodach Mhor,' Lachlan said with a little laugh.

I felt a fool, thinking of the miles that lay between us and the Bodach Mhor and the steep climb I would have after that to reach the cave where they meant to hide me – *if* I went with Lachlan at all! I turned determinedly towards him.

'I am not running away, Lachlan, till I know what is going on between you and Katrine and Peter Ross. What bargain has been struck? What has it to do with me?'

Lachlan sighed in exasperation. 'Connal, I swear to you that it has *nothing* – nothing at all to do with your being sought by the Sheriff. Will you believe me? Or do I have to force you to save yourself?'

He would not lie to me, I knew. Unwillingly I told him I was ready to go, and kept down behind him as he ran crouching towards the cover of the dry-stone wall that ran from our house down to the river.

'They have constables guarding the eastern approach to the townships,' Lachlan said hurriedly as we crouched down in the wall's shelter, 'and there are others placed at vantage points all around in case anyone tries to escape while they are searching the houses. The bed of the river is the only safe route westwards.'

He moved off again and I followed him along the line of the wall. Our next piece of cover after that was between two long, low lines of peats stacked ready for carting up to the townships. We had to bend almost double to move unseen between these lines and my broken shoulder ached abominably.

'We will have to crawl now,' Lachlan said over his shoulder as we came to the end of the peats. He pointed to the long shallow declivity of the drainage ditch that led down to the river, and added, 'Brace one foot hard against each side of the ditch and get as much forward leverage from that as you can. It will save your shoulder a little.'

I lowered myself into the ditch and, like a swimmer performing a side-stroke, I clawed forward with my one good hand while I pushed my feet hard against the sides of the ditch. Lachlan, wriggling along in front of me, was handicapped by his load but he still made such good progress that I had to strain every aching sinew to keep up with him.

'Tell me if I am going too fast for you,' he called softly back to me when we were half-way along the ditch, but I was determined not to admit the effort the pace was costing me and I only grunted in reply. It was a dear price I paid for my pride, however, for by the time I had slid after Lachlan down the culvert's last short slope to the river's edge and followed him a few yards along the bank, the pain in my shoulder had risen to such a peak that I fainted clean away.

I came back to my senses slowly, feeling bewildered at finding myself lying on the shingle of the river-bank with the front of my clothes all wet and muddy. Then, as the pain in my shoulder hit me again, I cried out and Lachlan clapped his hand across my mouth with a fierce whisper of warning. Lying close to me, he put his mouth to my ear and muttered, 'There is someone coming along the bank towards us. I am going to drag you under the overhang there. Brace yourself!'

I did as he told me, summoning all my will-power not to utter a sound as he gripped me round the waist and pulled me over himself so that I came to rest again with a broad grassy shelf of bank overhanging me. Lachlan rolled after me and we lay close together under the bank listening to the faint thud of footsteps overhead growing rapidly louder till they stopped a few yards from us.

We could hear voices, two of them, but it was not possible to make out what was said. The voices rumbled on, then one set of footsteps only came nearer to us and stopped right overhead. The soft wet earth of the bank above us came down in a trickle on our faces as the man standing there stamped a foot hard down on it.

'It is good land, see!' he called out to the other, unseen figure. 'Good, rich land,' and I recognized the thick, drawling voice of Sheriff-Officer Dugald McCaig.

The footsteps of the other man came towards us as McCaig spoke and he, too, stamped on the bank. The loosened earth came down in a shower on our faces with this, and I had to put a hand quickly over my mouth and nose to prevent myself spluttering. I looked over my hand at Lachlan and saw his eyes wide with apprehension.

'The ditch,' he mouthed silently at me, and I realized he was thinking of the trail our dragging bodies had left clearly marked along the line of the drainage ditch.

McCaig and the other man were still in conversation, and they seemed to be enjoying themselves for there were bursts of laughter from them every now and then. I held my breath, willing them not to move the extra few yards that would allow them to see the trail we had left, but with little real hope that our luck would hold so far.

It was the sound of a whistle from the direction of the townships that saved us. As it shrilled out, the second man swore and said, 'There goes the signal for the prisoner's escort.'

McCaig laughed at his annoyance and offered to go back to the schoolhouse with him. Lachlan waited till the sound of their retreating footsteps had died away then he wriggled out of cover and peered cautiously over the bank. I called softly up to him, 'What did they mean by "prisoner's escort"?'

Lachlan dropped down beside me again. 'They must have detailed that fellow off to take Peter back to Tain with him while they attend to the searching.'

I began to struggle to my feet and he gripped me firmly with one hand under my undamaged shoulder.

'Can you go on?'

'You promised that the search for me had nothing to do with Peter,' I mumbled.

'And I spoke the truth,' Lachlan retorted with a curtness that stilled any further argument from me. 'See if you can walk now.'

I stepped forward unsteadily, and with his hand still strongly supporting me we began the difficult journey along the rocky side of the river-bed. The banks on either side were high enough to allow us to walk upright without being seen from the road or from the townships, so that once I got over my first unsteadiness we made reasonable time. Lachlan kept encouraging me with reminders that we could take to the road again once we were out of sight of the constables patrolling it, and of those watching from the townships. I only nodded in reply to him for I was afraid that if I opened my mouth at all I would disgrace myself by giving voice to the groans of pain I kept biting back. We caught an occasional sight of the patrolling constables, but the bends and twists of the river gave us ample warning and time to crouch down out of sight till the danger had passed.

When Lachlan judged it safe for us to do so, we forded the river and climbed out on to the road. It was still rough going then, but even so, it was still much easier on my shoulder than all the slipping about and stumbling over rocks we had left behind us. I fell easily into the rhythm of the pace Lachlan set, and as we jogged on mile after mile the biting pain in my shoulder settled down until I had only a dull, steady ache to remind me of its condition.

It was the respite before the final test of the climb up the mountainside. I realized this as I looked up at the great escarpment of the Bodach Mhor towering over us at last in the day's fading light, and I was tempted to protest to Lachlan that I could not attempt the climb to the cave after all I had already endured. He started up the mountainside, however, without a backward glance at me, and there was nothing I could do except to follow where he led.

I put my feet where he had stepped, gripped where he gripped, blindly following the trail he marked out for me. There was a strange compulsion about the steadily-moving figure in front of me. So long as it kept climbing and gripping I had to force myself to climb and grip in imitation of it, in spite of the haze of weakness and pain that enveloped me.

All sense of distance and time left me. I was in an endless nightmare of painful movement that went on and on, till suddenly I found my feet on level ground and felt Lachlan's arm round me supporting me forward a few steps and then easing me down to sit on something flat and hard.

It was dark. One moment I could see nothing, the next, a light flared suddenly in the gloom. I blinked my way out of the daze that held me and recognized the rocky walls of the Bodach Mhor cave. Lachlan was bending over me with a small bottle of dark-green glass in his hand. He put it to my lips.

'I could not give you this earlier in case you fell asleep before the journey was over,' he said. 'Drink it now. It will ease the pain.'

He tilted the bottle so that I could swallow. The bitter taste of laudanum trickled into my mouth. I swallowed it and Lachlan eased me off the rocky shelf where I sat, on to something soft and blessedly comfortable. I closed my eyes and sighed.

Sleep! If I could only sleep and forget about the pain! Sleep – if only I could sleep . . .

I opened my eyes again on fire-light darting long red tongues up through the gloom of the cave. Lachlan was outlined against the light, his back towards me as he crouched over the fire burning in a hollow of the cave's floor. A big iron pot hung low from a tripod straddling the flames, and he was stirring slowly at its contents. I blinked at the sight of him and my mind struggled into full wakefulness. But for a few minutes at least, I was content to lie and look around me without speaking.

I was not the first one in Greenyards to escape capture by hiding in the Bodach Mhor cave. The place had been known to every generation that had lived in the glen and many a one before me had fled up the mountainside to its safety. The evidence of their occupation lay all around me – in the two horn spoons and bowls laid neatly on a rock shelf, in the pot swinging over the fire, in the deerskin couch under me. I could lie here in safety as long as I wished, for none but the people of Greenyards knew of the cave's existence and we were not given to telling our secrets to outsiders.

I turned my eyes back to Lachlan and tried to speak to him

but it was only a croak that came out of my mouth. Lachlan rose as the sound of it broke the stillness, and stepped over to me. He felt the pulse of my wrist, laid a hand on my brow for a moment, and then he said approvingly, 'You are better. You will be able to eat now, and high time too. It is nearly daylight.'

He went back to the fire, and while he was taking the two bowls from the shelf and ladling some stuff into the pot from them, I struggled into a sitting position on my pile of deerskins. Lachlan came over and handed one of the bowls to me.

'Porridge,' he said. 'Good stuff, with the meal mixed thick enough to stand the spoon upright in it. There is milk too, see, for I managed to catch one of our own ewes that had dropped twin lambs still-born, and she crying out for milking, poor creature.'

I looked into the bowl with some distaste for I had never seen milk actually poured on to porridge before, our custom being to have a separate bowl for each and to sup cleanly from them in turn. Lachlan grinned at my expression.

'There is a shortage of bowls,' he pointed out. 'Eat it up and be thankful I have not given it to you with sugar on it as well as milk, the way Englishmen eat it!'

The notion of sugar on porridge was so comical that I could not help grinning too, little though I believed that even Englishmen would so destroy the taste of good porridge. I took a few spoonfuls, and the hot, salty meal washed down by the milk brought back my voice to me.

'You have still to tell me why Peter Ross gave himself up to the Messenger-at-Arms,' I reminded Lachlan.

'The Sheriff sent the Messenger to propose a bargain,' he told me through mouthfuls from his own bowl. 'He offered to let three of the women arrested go free again in exchange for a man he could bring to trial as the ring-leader of the "riots".'

The spoon slipped from my hand. 'Which three? Is my mother among them?'

Lachlan shook his head. 'I am sorry, Connal.'

I bit back my disappointment as best I could, and when I could trust my voice again I asked:

'But why should the Sheriff want a man? What reason —?'

'Oh, think, Connal! Think!' Lachlan interrupted impatiently. 'His temper has cooled enough by this time to let him see how weak his case would be if it was only women he could bring to trial. He needs a man in the dock because only a man could be accused of offering a violent enough resistance to provoke the force his constables used.'

Fiercely then I demanded, 'And why should we sacrifice a man to make the Sheriff's case for him?'

'Because we must save these three women if we can,' Lachlan told me curtly, 'and because, if one man does not go willingly, the Sheriff will send to arrest as many as he can lay hands on and so leave the other women in worse case than before.'

'But why Peter? Why should Peter Ross be the one to take the blame? Rory Ruadh was the leader, if anyone was.'

'Peter made the choice himself,' Lachlan said. 'He will leave less heart-break behind him than any other man who might be taken, he said, for his wife is dead and he has no children.'

There was a pause and then he added, 'As for Rory, he is in military custody now and if we were to accuse him as the ringleader he would be tried by the Army as well as by the civil court. You know as well as the rest of us what the outcome of that would be.'

'He would be hanged under military law if they could prove such a charge against him!'

The words came out of me in little more than a whisper for it was only then that I realized the full horror of the situation the Sheriff's choice had laid on the people of the glen. One man must face an unknown penalty or another man would die. It was as simple and terrible as that.

'Rory left money with Katrine —' I began, and Lachlan

interrupted, 'I know. She is giving it to pay the lawyer Rory engaged for your mother to defend Peter also, and the rest of us will make up the sum that is needed. And there, for the time being at least, we must leave that matter and come back to yourself.'

He rose and laid another peat on the fire. 'You will have milk enough,' he said. He nodded towards the great boulder outcrop that almost blocked the cave's entrance and concealed its situation from outside. 'There is the little ewe tethered on a long rope so that she can graze.'

I followed his look and saw the dim white blur of the ewe crouched down in the rock's shelter, and Lachlan went on:

'There is a good supply of meal kept dry in the stone crock, there, by those who have been here before you. There is salt beef, bannocks and cheese in the bundle Katrine prepared for you. And water, of course, you can get from the torrent tumbling over the rock-face just outside the cave. I brought forward a good supply of peats for you from the back of the cave while you slept —'

'How long did I sleep?'

'The whole night – and now it is broad daylight and I must be gone in case there is a guard posted in the schoolhouse, and he maybe wondering why the medical student who looked after the women has suddenly vanished. Besides, there is a storm blowing in from the east, and if there is snow in it I may be trapped here for days.'

He walked to the boulder outcrop and stood beside it looking down the mountain. The little ewe rose from her crouched position and nuzzled against his leg. He bent down to stroke her head and murmur to her, and then he turned back into the cave saying: 'Be prudent in moving your shoulder till the bones are better knit, Connal. We will keep you supplied with food and send you word as soon as it is safe to come home.'

He paused and I waited, knowing that there was something

yet more important to say. It came at last as he reached into his pocket and drew out, first my pistol, and then the bag of powder and shot.

'Katrine took them from your jacket pocket while you were ill,' he said slowly. 'She gave them to me to keep and said you must not have them again, yet I cannot leave you here unarmed against the possibility of a blackguard like McCaig hunting you down. It would not be right.'

I held out my hand. 'I am grateful to you,' I told him, but Lachlan drew the pistol and bag back out of my reach.

'Remember how far the sound of a shot will carry,' he warned. 'You must use it only if your life is otherwise threatened.'

'I will remember,' I told him, and Lachlan dropped the pistol and powder bag into my outstretched hand.

He was almost gone before it struck me that there had not been a word of complaint about himself and his own plight from beginning to end of the affair. And realizing suddenly that the end of our livelihood in the glen meant that there would be no more money to pay for his University education, I called after him:

'Lachlan! What will happen to you? What are you going to do with yourself now?'

He looked back at me so briefly that I could not make out the expression on his face.

'There is always plenty of scavenging work to be picked up around the University classrooms and the hospital wards,' he said. 'You would be surprised at the amount of instruction in anatomy an attentive corpse-carrier could achieve if he listened hard enough: I'll save my wages from such work, Connal, and then take my degree in spite of Sheriff Taylor and his like!'

With a little laugh and a wave of his hand on the last words, he was gone. I laid the pistol on a stone in front of me. The fire-light gleamed red on the silver chasing of the stock and I leaned back against the wall of the cave watching it and thinking my own thoughts.

All day I sat there, moving only to put more peats on the fire or to drink occasionally from the pitcher of water Lachlan had put beside me. All day the storm blew up over the mountainside till it reached a pitch of fury in which it seemed that the mighty rock-bastion of the Bodach Mhor itself must crack and crumble before its onslaught. And all day the long black barrel and the silver mounting of the pistol gleamed and winked at me in the fire-light.

I could not take my eyes off it in the end.

My great-great-grandfather had charged with that pistol in his hand at the battle of Culloden, I thought. Firing it with his left hand, whirling his broadsword in his right, while the pipes screamed their war-rant, he had rushed forward in the great wave of Highlanders that charged into the murderous grape-shot of the English cannon. And with the dead from that charge piled breast-high on the field, broadsword and hand together shot away and only the pistol left to him, he had been hunted like a deer through the heather by the sabres of Hawley's Dragoons.

A year he had been in hiding after that while Butcher Cumberland's men burned and looted and murdered their way across the Highlands – a year, and the pistol had never left his grasp. Then the English Parliament had taken over the Butcher's work and completed it with their cruel laws. The pistol had been hidden in the thatch, and there it had stayed waiting the day of a rising that never came.

For the clans had made their last charge at Culloden. The power of their chiefs was broken and the sons who became chiefs after them were greedy for the new power that money could bring them. They sold the land that was the livelihood of their clans to sheep-men. The sheep-men came backed with the cannons and muskets of English soldiery to drive the people out, and the Culloden pistol was silenced for ever.

All the weapons that had spoken at Culloden had been silenced. Only here and there had a shot been fired, a sword swung suddenly against the invading sheep-men, but the people had submitted to their fate in the end. Leaderless since their chiefs had deserted them, weaponless since the law had forbidden them to carry arms, what choice had they but to submit?

So my reason argued with me, but there was a stronger force than reason working inside me as I stared at the pistol, for it seemed to me then that the glimmer and wink of its metal was like a challenge – a challenge to me to take hold of it and prove there was still one person in Greenyards who dared to defy the power of the English law.

I reached out to the pistol and picked it up, and with the feel of it in my hand the spark of my great-great-grandfather's final defiance of the Sheriff of his day leaped over the years and lit a small flame in my own mind. I stroked the pistol's smooth, cold barrel. I cocked the hammer and clicked the trigger, and I dreamed – hard, bitter dreams, of resistance and revenge. And so at last, while the storm still raged and battered at the mountain above me, I fell asleep, my hand under the deerskin pillow still clutching the pistol and my finger curled round the trigger.

There was a slackening off in the storm by the time I awoke. I tried my feet, and when I found I could move around without too much discomfort I began to set up some sort of life for myself in the cave. Sionaidh, the little ewe, bleated at me to be milked and afterwards she trotted at my heels as I cautiously took the air. From the mouth of the cave she watched me as I cooked for myself and tidied my bed of skins and blankets and, satisfied at last that she would not try to go off on her own again, I released the tethering rope and was pleased to find her that evening grazing contentedly near at hand. And waking later that night to feel an unexpected warmth I reached out and found her lying beside me, her fleece soft under my hand and her breath moving light and sweet-smelling against my cheek.

We came to know one another well, little Sionaidh and I, for it was another four days before I had the first visitors to my cave and during that time I talked to her of our troubles as if she had been another human being. Indeed, I was starved of human companionship, but nevertheless, when I first heard footsteps and voices below the cave I still crouched down with my pistol pointed at the entrance and the hammer drawn back to the firing position.

The sound of a familiar voice hailing me stilled my fears. I uncocked the pistol and thrusting it into my belt I ran from the cave to meet Mr. Aird coming towards me, his hand outstretched in greeting. I saw Katrine, with Murdo Ross and his cousin Angus each burdened with a pack, still toiling up the last hundred yards below us and then Mr. Aird was clasping my hand warmly and saying:

'Connal! I am sorry, my boy, more sorry than I can say that I could not be back in time to try and prevent that beastly affair at the boundary! No one in Glasgow could think or talk of anything except this Crimean War that has broken out – there are many Scots regiments involved, you know – and it was days before I could see the editor of the newspaper that employs Donald Ross, my journalist friend. And now —'

He stopped and half-turned to look down at Katrine. She was near enough then for me to see the tears that streaked her face. I looked quickly at Mr. Aird. He said in a whisper, 'Your grandfather.' I ran to Katrine and clasped hold of her and she leaned against me weeping.'

'Grandfather is dead, Connal. He is dead!'

I had not expected this, even though he was so weak when I

left him, for I could not imagine life without the quiet, kindly presence of old Donald Ban. The tears prickled suddenly under my eyelids and I drew Katrine's head down to my shoulder to hide my own heart's soreness from her.

Mr. Aird said, 'Try to think of it in this way, Connal. He was an old man and near his time. He would have had to go soon, anyway.'

'You would not have said that the night of the schoolhouse meeting when he stood up tall and straight as a pine-tree to make his speech to us,' I told him fiercely, 'so do not expect me to think like that now. It was not age that killed my grandfather, reverend sir. It was the blows of English batons on his skull and the shock to his spirit to see his own women-folk beaten like mad dogs!'

Murdo and Angus put down their burdens as I spoke. Murdo looked at me as if I had gone off my head to speak to the minister so, but his cousin Angus, being two years older, had the courage and the sense to speak out in agreement with me.

'Connal is right, Mr. Aird,' he said, 'and so is your journalist friend when he says that no words are strong enough to condemn the Sheriff's attack on us.'

I turned swiftly to Mr. Aird. 'So he has come back to the glen with you! Can he help us – *will* he help us to obtain justice?'

'He is doing everything he can,' Mr. Aird said. 'He has questioned everyone in the townships who was on the scene of the attack and has put their evidence into proper legal order in the form of sworn affidavits. Moreover, he has obtained testimony to their injuries from the doctors in Tain, and he has collected every scrap of physical evidence he could find – all the broken batons, the blood-stained caps and kerchiefs of the women, even the bloodied hanks of hair that were so brutally torn from poor Margaret Munro's scalp.'

'And the newspapers will publish all this?' I persisted. 'He will get them to raise an outcry on our behalf despite this war that has happened between England and Russia?'

Mr. Aird sighed. 'That is the trouble still, I am afraid. Space in the newspapers is at a premium just now, even in the great liberal newspapers that would otherwise have been prepared to champion our cause. However, if Donald Ross cannot obtain space in the public Press, he is determined to write a pamphlet on the facts and publish it at his own expense.'

'I am coming back with you to Greenyards then!' I told the minister exultantly. 'If there is still hope of justice then there is work to be done and I must share it.'

'*No!*'

They all said it at once, and while I stared at them in amazement over the chorus of denial, Katrine said to Murdo and Angus:

'Put the food in the cave for him and then wait farther down the mountainside for us.'

They moved away, casting curious backward glances at me. Katrine said quietly, 'Connal, even if Donald Ross does succeed in publishing his pamphlet, it will come too late to save us. Gillanders has set a date – the 15th of May – for taking possession of Greenyards. Our stock is to be sold at valuation then, and ourselves driven out. Those of us who can raise the passage-money will have to emigrate for there will be nowhere for us to go then but to the Americas.'

'You and I cannot emigrate,' I protested. 'We cannot leave the country and our mother in gaol awaiting trial!'

'No, we cannot go till the date is set for her trial and the outcome of it decided,' Katrine agreed. 'After that, we will see. And in between the date of the eviction and the time of the trial I will have to live wild here on the mountain with you. I will have no other place to live, and besides, the time of waiting may not be so bad for us if we are together.'

Angus and Murdo came out of the cave and went past us, waving and calling back a farewell as they scrambled down the mountainside. I hardly noticed them go, I was so taken up in my conversation with Katrine.

'But why cannot I come back with you to Greenyards, at least until the 15th of May?' I asked, and when she did not answer immediately I turned to Mr. Aird and told him angrily, 'I am not going to do what she says just because she is older than me! *I* am the one who is head of the family now that we have no men-folk left to us, and I say that I am coming home to Greenyards to bury my grandfather. It is my Christian duty to do so.'

'It would be, in other circumstances,' Mr. Aird said gravely, 'and it will count to your credit in the end that you were aware of it. Meantime, Katrine wishes to tell you herself why you must stay here, and when she has done so, remember that I will pray for you. And you, my boy, you must pray also for yourself for you will be walking very close to death from now on.'

He raised his hand briefly in blessing and turned to move slowly towards the boys waiting for him farther down the mountain. I looked in bewilderment at Katrine and found her watching me with compassion in her face.

'I remember from the time you were a little wee boy you never flinched from any danger however frightened you were,' she said quietly, 'and so I think you will bear what I have to say as bravely as you must.'

She waited, but I stayed silent and kept my face as expressionless as the sudden fear knocking at my ribs would allow. Katrine began speaking again.

'You will be arrested the moment you show face in Greenyards again, Connal,' she said. 'There are constables waiting there day and night for that purpose, for the day after you fled with Lachlan there was a proclamation posted against you. It says you are wanted for the attempted murder of an officer of the Queen's forces in the execution of his duty.'

I stared at her, stupefied for a moment. Then I understood and in a burst of angry protest I shouted, 'How can they accuse me of trying to murder McCaig! It was he who drew first – he who threatened to shoot my mother, the filthy, lying —'

I spluttered, unable to continue for the wrath that was choking me. I had grown used to the idea that McCaig's vengefulness over the pistol incident might lead to several years in gaol for me if I was caught. But this was different! This was a deliberate manufacture of a capital charge against me. They would *hang* me for this!

'Calm yourself, Connal,' Katrine broke into my splutterings. '*We* know that McCaig has lied! *We* know that the charge is not true, but they will try you on it all the same if you are caught, and attempted murder of a Sheriff-Officer is a hanging charge. Do you not see that? You *must not* be taken, Connal!'

In her exasperation at what she took for my slowness in understanding the position, she caught hold of me and shook me.

'Take your hands off, Katrine!' I told her angrily. 'I see very well how I am placed and I have no intention of letting myself be taken.'

Katrine sighed in relief. 'Thank heaven! Thank heaven you are being sensible.'

Then she noticed the pistol sticking in my belt and her eyes widened in dismay. I drew a step back from her and laid my hand on the butt of the pistol.

'Yes, I have it, and I will not be parted from it again,' I told her grimly. 'And when they do try to take me, you can depend on it that they will not succeed till I have first killed Sheriff-Officer Dugald McCaig!'

9 Why should I give myself up?

I was alone on the mountain after that except for brief visits from the young people of the townships who took it in turn to keep me supplied with food. They brought me tools also and so I had little time to brood for I had plenty of work to do in preparing the cave for Katrine's coming.

My injured shoulder forced me to work slowly but I still managed to fashion snares for grouse and hare as well as contriving some extra furnishings for the cave. I even began work on a spinning-wheel to replace the one Katrine would have to leave behind her when the time came.

By the end of April I had made the cave into a snug dwelling-place for the two of us. The weather held open and mild all this time so that I was able to work outside the cave, but with the first week in May came snow – the cuckoo-snow, as we call it, since it always comes to us with the first calling of the cuckoo each year.

At first it was only a few flakes drifting on a suddenly icy wind, but as the days passed the falls grew heavier and I had to spend more and more time inside the cave. Outside, the snow lay unmelting on the frost-hardened ground. All sound was muffled by it and in the stillness of the cave I grew sleepy sitting alone by the peat-fire. I began to lose track of the days that had still to pass till the evictions so that I was taken by surprise when Katrine eventually did arrive.

It was late one afternoon as I sat nodding by the fire that she appeared at the mouth of the cave. I jumped to my feet expecting some sort of outburst from her, some tears that would have to be comforted, but Katrine only stood there dry-eyed and shivering. I tried to draw her towards the fire but she stayed rigid in my grasp and began to speak rapidly in a low, toneless voice.

'They came early this morning – men with dogs and guns and torches. There were drovers with them, Englishmen and Lowlanders with loud voices and money jingling in their pockets. The cattle were auctioned off to them. The men with the torches set fire to the houses while the bidding went on. They levered off the roof-beams with crow-bars to make the wood burn faster.'

'Were any of the people hurt?' I asked anxiously, and in the same flat voice Katrine said:

'Some were – the sick, the elderly and the very young. Those who could not get quickly enough away from the flames. They suffered burns, and bruises from falling beams. And some of the women who were seized by a kind of madness that would not let them believe they were losing their homes had to be dragged out by the wreckers. They were not gently handled.'

'But there were no more deaths?'

'Old Phemy Munro – you know, Hugh's widow – I think she will die by nightfall.'

The steady toneless flow of Katrine's speech faltered and for the first time she looked directly at me.

'They would not give our men time to carry the poor crippled creature out in a blanket as they begged to be allowed to do. They slung her out in the snow like a heap of old clothes.'

The shivering that gripped Katrine became uncontrollable as she spoke of old Phemy. I seized her by the shoulders and pulled her forcibly over to the fire. I sat her down beside it, draped blankets round her, chafed her hands and then gave her some hot milk to drink.

While she drank I said: 'Now listen, Katrine, you are not to speak any more of it – not till the shock of it has passed a little. You will only upset yourself. You understand?'

She lowered the cup and looked at me, her eyes huge and dark in the drawn whiteness of her face.

'I will not cry over it,' she said bitterly. 'If you had seen what I have seen today, you would know how useless tears are now.'

I wished then that she *would* weep. Any outburst would have been better than the frozen, tearless face she turned on me. I sat poking at the fire and wondering awkwardly what I could say to comfort her but all I could think of was old Phemy Munro lying crippled and helpless outside her burning house.

'Well, it is all past, Katrine,' I said when I could bear the silence no longer. 'You will be safe up here with me now, and maybe even happy again for I have made the cave fine and comfortable for you.'

I searched her face, hoping for a smile. 'You'll see,' I promised, 'the pair of us will live up here till the trial as if we were king and queen of the mountain!'

'A fine king and queen!' Katrine said. There was a little catch in her voice as she spoke and she looked at me with an expression on her face I could not fathom. She said no more, however, and so I began to show her all the things I had made to let her see the fine life we could lead up there on the Bodach Mhor. She looked and listened, but there was no smile from her then or for many days afterwards.

It was only a week later when the snow melted in a warm west wind and she was able to come out and about with me that she began to return to the sort of person she had been.

I did my best to fan the little spark of returning liveliness in her, showing her how to lay the snares I had made, and later, how to fashion more of them. I took her with me at night when I went stealthily to raid the secret stores of food laid down by Rory Ruadh's 'iron-ration brigade'. Together we searched the corries for the survivors of the little flock of ewes we had turned loose, clipped their fleeces and sat in the sun carding the wool for her to spin on the wheel I had made. Neither of us had ever lived soft before and this was a harder way of life than anything we had ever known, but Katrine seemed to thrive on it and by the middle of June she was her normal, sensible self again.

As for myself, although my shoulder continued to trouble me, I grew lean and hard and brown as an Indian with all the hunting and trapping I had to do to keep us in fresh meat. I learned to go so cat-foot-quiet through the heather that I could creep up on a sitting grouse and clutch her before she went cackling off her nest. My sight sharpened with constant scanning of far spaces till I could have matched it with that of an eagle, and if McCaig had been with any of the patrols I saw occasionally in the floor of the valley I could have had a bead drawn on him before he caught the flick of my foot through the heather.

I never let matters come to this pass, however, but always went quietly roundabout back to the cave to warn Katrine not to show herself till the patrol had passed by.

This sort of situation also, Katrine took in good part – better than myself in fact, for while she remained calm at these times I was always tense and uneasy till it was quite certain that the patrol had no idea of where we were hidden. Indeed, I marvelled sometimes at her calmness and at the other ways in which she refused to yield to our circumstances, for while I grew daily more unkempt in my appearance she somehow managed to keep herself as neat as she had always been.

Katrine nagged me about the way I looked. She kept telling me I was like a proper wild man of the mountains and that if it was not for her care the cave would always be in a mess of skins and traps and other hunting gear.

'Just a mess, a proper *bourach*, that is what it would be,' was her constant cry, but I only grinned when she said this and thought to myself that I would rather have a scold for an elder sister than the subdued, shivering girl she had been on the day of the burnings.

We did not speak of that day again, but we often discussed the business of our mother's trial. It was to be some time in the autumn we knew from a letter sent by Hector Cameron, the lawyer, to Katrine just before she joined me in the cave. There had been no other word of our mother in the letter, however, and as the time passed we grew so anxious to have news of her that Katrine decided to go into Tain and see what she could find out.

She left the cave at dawn one day at the end of June, for it would take her an entire day to walk the long distance into Tain. I let her go with many misgivings, and spent that day and the next forty-eight hours biting my nails with anxiety for her safety. I also kept constant watch in the daylight hours in case she was followed back to the cave, and at night I slept with my pistol close to my hand.

It was late in the evening of the third day that she appeared again. She was clearly exhausted by the effort of the double journey but the food I had ready put new life in her. She talked as she ate, telling me that the trial had been arranged to take place on the 14th of September before Lord Justice Clerk Hope in the Northern Circuit Court at Inverness Castle. Meanwhile, she said, our mother and Peter Ross were well and were being reasonably well treated in gaol.

'They would only let me stay with her for half an hour,' she went on. 'She said little in that time – her manner is become very subdued, Connal – but she was very definite that you and I must find a new life for ourselves in the Americas when the trial is over, and that you must keep well hidden till then.'

'And what of her chances? Is Hector Cameron as good a lawyer as they say he is?'

'Oh, he is shrewd, very shrewd indeed,' Katrine assured me. 'She could not be in better hands.'

We talked of this for a while and then she went on to tell me the news that Mr. Cameron had passed on to her about Donald Ross, the journalist.

'The editors he approached thought he must be exaggerating the case,' she said, 'for Sheriff Taylor had already given them an account of the attack that said the men of Greenyards rioted against his constables so that they had to charge in self-defence. Then, according to the Sheriff, our men ran away leaving the women to take the brunt of the charge.'

'But Donald Ross said he would publish the truth at his own expense if the newspapers failed him,' I reminded her.

'And so he has,' Katrine informed me, 'and he has even written a letter to the Lord Advocate himself. But I doubt it will be of little use, Connal. People in the south have no knowledge of the way things are here, and so the story Sheriff Taylor gave to the newspapers is the one they will choose to believe.'

I had never felt so lonely as I did listening to Katrine then, and if it had not been that she needed me I think I would have gone off to Tain there and then and challenged Sheriff Taylor and Dugald McCaig to their lying faces. I said so to Katrine and she flared up at me:

'You are never to talk like that again! Do you hear? You must promise – promise me, Connal, you will never give yourself up!'

'Are you mad, Katrine? Why should I give myself up? I meant only that I would like to take my pistol and —'

I stopped short, arrested by the look of dismay on Katrine's face.

'Why do you think I would give myself up?' I asked quietly. 'You have gone very red all of a sudden, Katrine. What are you hiding from me?'

'I am hiding nothing,' Katrine insisted. 'I will not have you talking such childish nonsense, that is all.'

She was suddenly very much my elder sister again, and I the young brother she had alternately bullied and petted as long as I could remember. I could get nothing more from her that night, and whenever I tried to open the subject again she brushed it aside with the lofty remark:

'You must leave all these matters to myself and Mr. Cameron now, Connal.'

I raged inwardly at being treated like this, as if I was a child without a mind of my own, and the more she tried to put me off the more convinced I became that she was holding back some new information concerning myself. Nothing I could think of fitted into the pattern of this suspicion, but still, I could not dismiss it from my mind.

I began to watch Katrine intently, to listen carefully for a hidden meaning in her words. And in my turn, I felt her watching me and weighing every word I said about the trial, or McCaig, or Sheriff Taylor. On the surface, everything between us was the same as it had been before she went to Tain, and we both pretended not to be aware of the current of mutual suspicion that dragged underneath our conversations. But it was there for both of us all the same, all through the months of July and August.

The pattern of our life changed but little in that time, except that with the heat of summer I grew lazier. As the blaeberries ripened on the slopes about the cave I was content to lie in the sun and pick at them till my hands and lips were stained purple with the juice, but Katrine gathered bowls full of them and scolded me for my laziness now as well as for my wild appearance.

'You are wasting your time gathering berries we will never eat,' I told her. 'The trial is only a week from now and after that we will be gone.'

To my utter astonishment then, Katrine sat down with the bowl of blaeberries in her lap and began to cry as if her heart would break. I let the worst of it pass and then I took the bowl from her and dried her tears.

'You had better tell me the truth,' I said. 'You have kept it to yourself long enough.'

'I tried,' Katrine said in a choked voice. 'I tried hard, Connal. It was you talking of the trial being so near at hand that broke me down.'

'And now —?' I prompted her.

She raised a tragic face to me. 'They are going to charge *her* with the crime you are accused of. They could not find you so they are going to fasten the charge of attempting to murder McCaig on to her instead.'

I could think of nothing to say. It was so unexpected, the ingenuity of it so fiendish! My mother to be made the scapegoat for *my* 'crime'!

I sat staring at Katrine and trying to grasp the enormity of the idea. She put her hands over mine and said timidly:

'You will not do it, will you, Connal? You will not give yourself up? They are only trying to flush you out of hiding, do you not see? That is why they are accusing her. They think that will make you give yourself up – to save her!'

'They reasoned well!'

I stood up, brushing berries and leaves away from myself.

'Pack what you need, Katrine. We are going into Tain now, together.'

'No, Connal, no!' She jumped to her feet, clutching at me. 'They will hang you!'

'They will hang her instead if I do not go,' I pointed out. I was cold, icy-cold with a kind of rage I had never felt before freezing all my thoughts into an ice-sharp clarity.

'Connal, listen to me,' Katrine said desperately. 'I kept my own counsel on this because I knew I could not hope to hold you here all summer once you knew the position. But it is not so hopeless as it seems. Mr. Cameron has a plan to save her.'

'Let Cameron try his plan,' I told her. 'I am for Tain and the Sheriff's office.'

'Speak to Mr. Cameron first,' Katrine begged. 'Only keep out of the Sheriff's way till you can speak secretly with Cameron. Please, Connal, please! I have stood by you till now. Do this one thing for me, please!'

I was touched by her pleading. It was not every girl who would have suffered such a rough life uncomplainingly, and softened by the thought, I promised her. Katrine immediately became practical again.

'Then we cannot leave for Tain until the morning,' she declared. 'We must arrive there during the night if you are to reach Mr. Cameron's house unseen.'

Grudgingly I agreed to this. We went back to the cave, and while Katrine prepared a bundle of food for the journey, I cleaned and reloaded my pistol. It was only a token gesture on my part, for now there would be no opportunity for the revenge I had planned on Dugald McCaig when he tried to arrest me. Sheriff Taylor's cunning had seen to that, I thought savagely, and wondered if either of them would ever guess that the Sheriff had turned the tables on me even more neatly than he had intended.

I found it hard to sleep that night. It was only lying in the darkness of the cave that I realized the full horror of what lay before me once I was in the clutches of the law. Not that I had ever seen a hanging. It was my imagination that supplied the

106

details which made me sweat and writhe against my pillow, and sent one ghastly vision after another floating in front of my eyes.

I felt the cold, harsh touch of the rope around my neck. I saw the hangman, black-hooded. I saw him raise his hood to reveal the gross, whiskered face of McCaig grinning at me before I dropped. I felt the rope jerk and tighten on my throat, the knot press like an iron fist into the artery below my ear. The blood pounded in my head. I kicked and gasped wildly for air. I was dying ... dying ... suffocating ... air ... I needed air in my lungs to scream ... scream ... scream ...

I woke, screaming, to the knowledge that I had dreamed it all. Katrine was kneeling beside me, her arms round me. I clutched at her and buried my face against her.

'I am afraid to go – I am afraid to die like that – Katrine, I am afraid!'

I was whimpering against her like a baby. She stroked my hair and soothed me, 'Husha, husha now, Conn, my little Conn. You are not going to die. Katrine is here. She will not let you die.'

Her voice murmured soothingly on in my ear and gradually I regained control of myself. I sat up, and putting her gently aside I made up the fire and crouched in front of it with a blanket pulled round my shoulders.

Katrine sat beside me. After a time she whispered, 'Do not go, Connal. You are too young for – that.'

'I must go,' I said quietly. 'I cannot let her die in my place.'

Katrine began to say something but I turned on her and asked fiercely, 'Could *you*? Could you stay here and know she was to die for you?'

Katrine shook her head and we sat silently together there till the morning.

At dawn we left the cave and worked our way eastwards down the glen, keeping to the high hill-paths in case we were

107

seen by the new tenants of Greenyards – the sheep-drovers. It was slow going, accordingly, but our pace picked up when we passed Ardgay and struck south-east to meet the coast-line of the Dornoch Firth.

I knew this part of the road well having driven cattle over it many a time to the market in Tain. I set a good pace down it, therefore, with little fear of being met or overtaken since the dusk was now coming down on us and the road was straight enough for me to have a good view before and behind. Katrine matched her pace to mine, and when I saw she had no difficulty in keeping up with me I gradually increased my speed till we were marching along at the military pace we had learned from Rory Ruadh.

It was dark by the time we reached the outskirts of the town. Katrine drew me to a halt and said:

'Go slowly when we reach the houses, Connal. Saunter along, and if you see anyone approaching put your arm round my waist and turn your face towards mine as if we were lovers making our way to a tryst.'

I grunted, thinking what a fool I should feel if I had to do any such thing, but fortunately there was no need for a ruse like this. The town was deserted at that hour, the house-fronts black and lifeless, and the only sound we heard was a dog howling mournfully, far off.

Katrine turned down a street that seemed to lead directly to the Firth, the water of it gleaming a brighter steel-grey at us the nearer we drew to it. Half-way down the street Katrine jerked my arm and pointed to a big house built solidly of stone, fronting on to the street and backed by a long strip of walled garden. To our left, a narrow lane ran along one side of the garden wall.

'There,' Katrine whispered. 'There is Cameron's house.' She pointed to the lane. 'Go down that lane a few yards then climb over the wall and hide in the garden. Give me time to

108

wake up Cameron and talk to him, then come up to the back door of the house. I will let you in.'

She squeezed my hand and turned away towards the front door of the house. I waited till she had raised the brass knocker and rapped on the door with it. The sound of it rang out with shocking loudness in the quiet of the street, and with the feeling that it would waken the whole town to our presence I ran quickly down the lane and climbed over the wall of Mr. Cameron's garden.

I landed in a bed of rose-bushes. Petals showered on me and thorns tore at my skin and clothes. I struggled to my feet, cursing the luck that had made me choose that spot to climb the wall, and disentangled myself from the clinging stems. There was a clump of tall shrubs near the rose-bed and I made for this. Katrine's knocking still came faintly to me as I crouched down behind the shrubs and I looked up at the house watching impatiently for a light to appear in it.

I saw one at last, a faint glow rapidly passing behind one of the darkened windows on the upper floor, and guessed at some-one – Cameron himself, I hoped – going candle-lit down the stairs towards the front door. I waited a few more minutes and then I ran, crouching, towards the house. I found the back door and waited beside it in the deep shadow cast by the house-wall.

Katrine must have been able to explain our visit very quickly for it was very soon afterwards that the door opened quietly and I saw her standing there with a candle in her hand. She beckoned me inside. I stepped over the threshold and closed the outer door noiselessly behind me.

Katrine moved ahead of me with her candle, through the kitchen premises and out into a long passage. At the end of the passage we went through a swing-door, down a shorter passage and then through another door that led into a large room furnished like an office with desks and stools.

There was a man standing in front of the empty fireplace in the room. He was of medium height and sparely built, with a ruddy, sharp-featured face. He was dressed in a night-shirt with a red, quilted bed-gown over it and his bare feet were thrust into slippers. A tasselled night-cap sat askew on his head and from under it his eyes regarded me curiously.

'Mr. Cameron,' Katrine said, 'this is my young brother, Connal.'

Cameron held out his hand to me. He had a dry and sinewy grip, which pleased me. I liked also the shrewd cast of his features, and the twinkle of humour in his eyes when he observed: 'I cannot say I am pleased to make your acquaintance, boy – not when you come in this fashion! But at least I am interested.'

He turned towards a big mirror fixed on the wall over the fireplace, and added: 'It strikes me you have not seen yourself lately, Connal Ross. Take a look in this mirror, will you?'

I stepped up to the mirror and looked into it, and was surprised and somewhat dismayed at the sight of myself. It was not only that my face was burned by the sun and stained purple around the mouth with blaeberry juice, or that the wild tangle of my hair fell nearly to my shoulders. I had become hollow-eyed, my cheeks lean and sunken beneath the ridges of my nose and cheek-bones, and the eyes staring at me from under the shadow of my brows were fierce and angry-looking.

Behind my back Cameron asked, 'How old are you, boy?'

I turned impatiently away from the mirror. 'Fifteen and six months. Does that matter now?'

111

'One of my sons is the same age,' Cameron said. 'He would look like a babe beside you.'

'He has not spent more than five months hunted for his life,' I answered sourly.

The humour vanished from Cameron's face. 'True, true,' he muttered. He stared thoughtfully at me, and then with a sudden briskness in his manner he waved a hand in the direction of the stools and commanded Katrine and myself to sit down.

'We must talk,' he said, 'or rather, I must talk and you must listen.'

'There is nothing to talk about, Mr. Cameron,' I said flatly. 'I am determined to give myself up.'

Cameron's eyes bored into mine. Slowly he said, 'Young man, *I* am defending this case. Pray allow me to speak to my plea before you lodge objections to it.'

His tone put me properly in my place and I mumbled an apology. Cameron inclined his head in a polite little nod of acceptance, then he went on:

'First, let us take the original charges that were laid against your mother – mobbing and rioting, and breach of the peace. It may be possible to have these all reduced to one lesser charge (you will see how presently), but do not deceive yourself for one moment that they can be set aside altogether. It is the law of property she has transgressed – a law more sacred in this country, and particularly in the Highlands, than all the Ten Commandments put together!

'Therefore, if the Sheriff is not to have the whole landowning aristocracy in the countryside up in arms and trying to unseat him from office, he *must* secure a conviction on the charges he prefers against your mother and Peter Ross. And, I must warn you, it is absolutely certain he will do so. Your mother's only plea that she was acting in defence of her own property-rights and not in defiance of a usurper's right to her home, was contained in that false assurance given by Alexander

Munro of Braelangwell – and, so far as we know, even that no longer exists. Furthermore, the jury at the trial will be a packed one entirely made up of these land-owning gentry whose power she has defied, and so they are bound to convict her.'

'Could we not appeal against the court's decision?' Katrine asked timidly.

'Litigation is an expensive course to pursue, my dear. Could you afford law costs that would run you into hundreds of pounds?'

Cameron's tone was kindly, but Katrine was so plainly discomfited by his words that I burst out angrily:

'Very well, you have shown us that we can do nothing against the charges you have named. But what of the other one – the charge of attempted murder? What do you say to that?'

'You take me up wrongly, boy,' Cameron said. 'I told you that we cannot have the charges of mobbing and rioting dismissed altogether, but we *can* do something about them. As to the other, graver charge, I think we can do much more, for it may be possible to make a bargain with the Sheriff to have it dropped completely from the indictment. He has already made one bargain with the people of Greenyards, after all, and a man who makes one bargain is usually open to suggestion over another.'

I slid down from my seat and faced up to Cameron. 'The Sheriff has already made it clear what bargain he will accept – myself for my mother! If I give myself up he will withdraw the charge of attempted murder against her.'

'No, no, no!' Cameron waved his hands at me in exasperation. 'That would be playing right into the Sheriff's hands. We can do better than that, my boy, much better. Now, listen. I have a meeting arranged with him for ten o'clock tomorrow morning. Sit down again and listen to the bargain *I* will propose.'

I went back to my seat. Cameron began to talk again, rapidly this time, pacing back and forward and waving his hands to emphasize each point in the plan he was expounding. I listened to him, fascinated, for there was no doubt it was an ingenious one and if it could be successfully carried off . . .

'You mentioned money,' I interrupted Cameron. 'The Sheriff will know we have not the money to carry through these proposals of yours.'

Cameron laughed. 'Will he? You leave that to me, boy. It will be my responsibility to convince him that we have.'

'Then you would have to tell a lot of lies,' Katrine objected.

'I am an elder of the Free Kirk, Miss Ross,' Cameron said in injured tones. 'I have never told a lie in my life!'

I laughed, I could not help it then. 'You will have to bend the truth more than a little, all the same, to get the Sheriff to agree to what you suggest.'

A smile quirked the corners of Cameron's mouth. 'Maybe, maybe,' he said, 'but I think he *will* agree.'

'Aye, maybe at the time,' I said, suddenly doubting. 'You might frighten him into agreeing at this meeting you say you are having tomorrow, but what happens in court could be a different story. You said yourself he dare not go against the gentry. What happens if he does not keep his bargain in court?'

Cameron shrugged and threw up his hands. 'We would be finished. He would have called our bluff.'

I rose to my feet again, determined not to be put down this time. 'I want to be at the trial, Mr. Cameron. I *must* be there.'

'Connal, how can you be so stupid!' Katrine jumped to her feet and thrust herself between us. I drew aside.

'Well, Mr. Cameron?'

'You would be recognized – arrested straight away,' Katrine protested again.

But Cameron said musingly, 'I am not so sure.'

He rubbed at his chin and looked me up and down. Then he walked round me, Katrine watching him in astonishment and dismay, myself in hope. When he came to a halt again, it was to Katrine he spoke.

'You see, Miss Ross, you cannot disguise a boy – except as a girl, maybe, but Connal is much too broad in the shoulders and big in the feet for that. What you *can* do, however, is to make him into *an entirely different kind of boy*!'

'Now, Mr. Cameron —' Katrine began, but Cameron ignored her and began rummaging under the lid of one of the desks.

'I know how it feels to be waiting at second-hand for news from a court-room,' he said, 'and if Connal has spirit enough to take the chance — Ah! Here they are!'

He drew his hand out from the desk flourishing a pair of scissors. 'Here, take these, Miss Ross, and clip that wild hair of his neat and close. And you, Connal, go through that door to the little room beside this office once you are cropped. You will find a basin, soap and water in there. Wash some of that mountain grime off you and while you are doing that I will be fetching you clothes to wear.'

Katrine took the scissors unwillingly from him. He flashed a look full of interest and amusement at me, and then hurried out of the room.

'Quickly, Katrine. Do as he says,' I told her. I was beginning to like Hector Cameron very much.

'You are mad, both of you,' Katrine said helplessly, but she began to cut my hair all the same and made a good job of it, too, as I saw when I looked in the mirror at the neat crop she had given me.

I went through the door Cameron had indicated then and found a little room laid out with a table holding a basin and a ewer of water. There was soap in a dish beside the ewer and towels on a rail. I washed my hands and face and was doing the same for my cropped head when there was a knock at the door of the little room. I heard it open and Cameron's voice behind me say, 'There is all you will need, boy,' and then there was the sound of the door closing again.

I turned from the basin, towelling my head dry. On a chair

115

behind me lay a suit of black broadcloth, beautiful smooth stuff, a shirt with a high, stiff collar, a silver-grey cravat, black stockings and boots. I turned them all over carefully, marvelling at the smooth rich feel of them all and wondering if they belonged to the son Cameron had said was the same age as myself.

They certainly fitted me, although the coat could have done with a bit more ease over the shoulders. The pistol did not show under it, however, any more than it had done under my old jacket, and I stepped back into the office wondering curiously how I would look to the other two. Katrine pounced on me immediately, holding out a comb and ordering me to comb my hair while Cameron stood back smiling and admiring his handiwork.

'Now do you see what I mean, Miss Ross?' he asked. 'Look at him! Can you imagine anything less like the tousled, hunted-looking creature who walked in here? There is no law-officer on the prowl would look twice at him now – except maybe to admire his clothes!'

There was no doubt that the change in my appearance was more effective than any disguise could have been. I looked smooth and elegant now, from my neatly-combed hair to the bright shine of my expensive boots the very picture of a well-to-do solicitor's clerk. The cropped hair and the high collar had altered the appearance of my face too. It was a lean, scholarly-looking face that gazed back at me from the mirror now, instead of a lean, wolfish-looking one.

'You had better sit in the gallery of the court,' Cameron said to my reflection. 'You will be farther away from the place where the Sheriff-Officers sit than in the public benches downstairs. Look, I will draw it out for you.'

He pulled a sheet of paper towards him and began to make a sketch of the court-room. Katrine and I both moved to look over his shoulder as he explained:

'This is the shape of the court, see – a circular room about forty feet across with a gallery running half-way round the upper part of the circle. The judge's chair stands on this raised part of the floor at the opposite side of the court from the gallery, and is separated from the well of the court by a panelled barrier. Here are the jury pews on the right of the court and the witness-box on the left. The dock stands here, in the centre of the floor of the court. And here, between the dock and the barrier in front of the judge's chair, is the solicitors' table. The Advocate Depute, who prosecutes for the Crown, will sit on the judge's right-hand side of this table, and I will be here on the left-hand side with Mr. Moncrieff, your Counsel.

'Why must we have this Mr. Moncrieff?' Katrine asked. 'Can you not speak for us, Mr. Cameron?'

'I could, but we must observe the normal procedures of the Court or risk censure from the Judge,' Cameron told her. 'And in any case, I think you will be satisfied with Moncrieff. He is young and so his fee is still moderate, but he is very eloquent.'

'Is it certain McCaig will attend the trial,' I asked, 'even if matters go as you plan and there are no witnesses called for the prosecution?'

'I should say he most certainly will,' Cameron answered. 'I cannot imagine such a vindictive man missing the slightest opportunity to gloat.'

'And what will happen if matters do *not* go as you plan? What happens if the Sheriff refuses this bargain you hope to make with him?'

'I told you,' Cameron said impatiently. 'We are finished if that happens.'

I straightened up from studying the sketch of the courtroom. 'Oh no, we are not, Mr. Cameron! If the Sheriff persists in the charge of attempted murder against my mother I will stand up in court and give myself up, as I intended to do in the first place. That is *why* I want to be there.'

'I see!' Cameron plucked thoughtfully at his long upper lip. 'And what makes you think either judge or jury will believe it was you who committed the crime for which another has been brought before them? *They* will not know that the Sheriff only charged your mother with it in the first place in order to flush you out of hiding. Nor will they know he has been forced to proceed with the charge against her because he failed in that purpose. You could tell them so, of course, but how could you convince them of the truth of your statement?'

Ignoring his questions, I asked one of my own. 'Where will McCaig be sitting at the trial?'

Cameron glanced at me, frowning, and then tapped the sketch. 'Here, on the Judge's left, in one of the chairs reserved for law-officers.'

I studied the place he had indicated and said, 'So if we sit in the gallery on the same side of the court as McCaig we would be out of the immediate range of his vision?'

'A casual glance from him would certainly not find you,' Cameron agreed. 'He would have to turn half-round and look upwards before he had a proper view of you. But even so, it is not likely he would recognize you as you are now. I would not agree to your being there if I thought otherwise.'

I nodded. 'Good! That is how I hoped matters would be. And now that we have settled those points, Mr. Cameron, I will show you how I will convince the Court, if need be, that they have the wrong person in the dock.'

I slid my hand inside my coat and drew my pistol, clicked back the hammer and pointed the weapon at Cameron.

'Like this!'

He gasped, and with the sweat starting out on his brow backed away from me. Katrine clutched at my arm. I brushed her aside and said to Cameron:

'I will have McCaig within range of this pistol, Mr. Cameron, and if my mother *is* accused of having attempted to murder him, I shall shoot him in open court in front of everyone. No false evidence against her will stand in face of that proof against me!'

'Give that thing to me at once,' Cameron commanded. 'I will desert your case if you do not! Do you hear, boy? Give me that pistol or find another lawyer.'

'Give it to Mr. Cameron, Connal,' Katrine pleaded. 'We cannot do without him now.'

I shook my head. 'I am sorry, Katrine. I am not going to run the risk of the Sheriff failing to keep his bargain.'

'There will be no bargain if you do not lay down that pistol,' Cameron said sharply, 'for I will wash my hands of the case!'

'You must do as your conscience dictates, Mr. Cameron,' I told him, 'and I must obey mine.'

Cameron glared at me. 'If you were my son,' he snorted, 'I would beat you for this!'

'If I were your son,' I told him quietly, 'the woman in the dock would be your wife as well as my mother. Would you beat your son then for taking a last desperate chance to save her?'

Cameron held me with his glare for a moment longer, then his eyes dropped from mine and he turned away, snatching off his night-cap and rubbing the sweat from his brow with it. He sat down with the crumpled night-cap squeezed between his hands, and looked slowly from Katrine to myself. I put the pistol away again, keeping my eyes on Cameron as I did so. His eyes dropped to follow the movement of my hand and then returned to glance at Katrine's anxious face.

'I should send you both packing now,' he said at last in a tired voice. 'God knows how this case will finish if I do not. I could be struck off the Roll of Solicitors – did you know that? – if I allowed a client to come armed into court.'

Neither Katrine nor I said anything. She was standing twisting her fingers nervously together but I felt quite calm for my decision was firmly taken now and I would not go back on it. I was determined not to trust the final swing of our fortunes to the twisted form of law practised by the Court which would try my mother. The pistol would be my law. One sure, steady shot from my pistol would see justice done at last – true justice.

And so I kept silent, though I could have argued it out in this way with Cameron, for it was in my mind that he knew my thoughts already and that was why he had not yet concluded his threat to abandon our case.

When Cameron spoke again it was only to mutter to himself, 'Heaven knows I am ready to take risks for a client, but this —'

He rose and began pacing up and down, leaving his sentence unfinished. He was beginning to waver, I thought. I caught Katrine's eye but she put a finger to her lips, warning me not to speak. Cameron came to a halt in his pacing and looked at me.

'How would you like,' he said slowly, 'to come with me to the Sheriff's office tomorrow?'

I would not like it at all, I thought, and told him so promptly. 'I have to take the chance of being recognized in the courtroom,' I pointed out. 'It would be doubling that risk unnecessarily to go to the Sheriff's office with you. I might even run into McCaig himself there, and he is the one most likely to recognize me. Why should I go?'

'Because it might make you abandon this mad idea of yours,' Cameron snapped. 'You would hear me talk to the Sheriff, hear me put the bargain to him and see how unlikely it is that he would try to go back on it.'

'And what if I am recognized there and arrested?' I asked, and Cameron answered me with another question.

'What if you are recognized there and *I* am struck off the Roll of Solicitors for harbouring a fugitive – as I could be this very minute for having you in my house?'

I had no reply to that. 'You see,' he said triumphantly, 'you want me to conduct your case and take all the risks for you, but *you* will take none on my behalf!'

I looked away from him in some confusion and Cameron pressed his advantage home. 'The Sheriff has never seen you except maybe to catch a glimpse of you in the crowd on the day of the attack on the women,' he said persuasively. 'It is only your description as McCaig gave it to him that he has to go on, and now you look totally different. Besides, it would be quite natural for me to be accompanied by a clerk and you look that part to perfection now. All you would have to do would be to sit in the background and pretend to take notes. Like this, see!'

He seized a note-pad from one of the desks and scribbled a quick series of strokes and flourishes on it. 'This is the speed-writing the reporters do in court,' he said, shoving the paper into my hands. 'You could imitate it – anyone can. Or are you too afraid to take even a shared risk with me?'

His words stung me even though I realized they were meant to do so. I threw the note-pad down on the desk.

'It will not make any difference to my intentions,' I told him coldly, 'but I will not have you say I backed down from a risk you were willing to take on my behalf. I will come with you tomorrow.'

'Without the pistol!' Cameron said quickly. 'I would be charged along with you if you were found carrying arms in the Sheriff's office.'

I stared suspiciously at him but his face showed only anxious concern. 'I would not only be struck off the Roll, I would finish up in gaol beside you,' he added. 'Would you have me risk that, also, for my fee?'

'You are not doing this much for us only to earn a fee, Mr. Cameron,' Katrine said quietly.

Cameron glanced quickly at her and then turned away to

lean on the desk, his face twisted as if in pain and his eyes staring blindly into the distance.

'No,' he said, 'it is not for the fee.' There was a long silence and then he looked up at Katrine again. 'You are only young, you and your brother. You have seen only one glen cleared to make way for sheep but I have seen it happen time and again. All the time I have practised law I have had a trail of miserable people pass through this office begging me to protect them from the monied land-grabbers of the South. But there *is* no justice for the poor Highlander whose only title to his land is a moral one. The law of property recognizes only title-deeds written on paper. It pays no heed to those granted by tradition and written in the blood of sacrifice, and I hate that law, Miss Ross. My blood is as Highland as yours and I hate the law that does such things to my people. That is why I am willing to take risks to help you. I have taken them for others in the past in like cases and I am willing to do so for you now – if your brother would only see reason.'

Katrine turned to me. 'Leave the pistol with me tomorrow,' she said. 'If Mr. Cameron is to continue our case it would be unfair to you both to increase the risks you would be taking then.'

'It is already tomorrow,' Cameron said. He twitched aside a curtain and pale light streamed into the room. Katrine held out her hand. She and Cameron waited, watching me, watching for my hand sliding under my coat to reach the pistol.

'Come along, boy. I will cover you if you have to make a run for it!'

I had been moved by Cameron's words but I was still reluctant to yield the pistol to him. Now the almost jeering note that had crept back into his voice had the opposite effect on me. In a spurt of anger that brought the blood rising swiftly to my face I snatched the pistol out of my belt and handed it, with the bag of powder and shot, to Katrine.

'There you are, Mr. Cameron,' I said defiantly. 'I am ready to face *your* risks on *your* terms.'

Cameron rubbed his hands and smiled at us both. 'Good, good! I knew that reason would prevail! And now that it has, we can get back to practical matters. You, Connal, will stay here till I am ready to go to the Sheriff's office. And you, Miss Ross, take this note to this address and stay there till Connal joins you again later in the day.'

Sitting down as he spoke, he wrote quickly and handed the note to Katrine. 'The good woman at this address runs a lodging-house,' he told her, 'a good one and cheap. She was nurse to my boys at one time and so she will take care of you and keep quiet about it for my sake.'

He rose from the desk. 'Come, my dear. I will escort you to the door.'

Katrine put the note along with the pistol and the ammunition into the pocket of her gown, and smiled uncertainly at me. 'Be careful, Connal,' she said, and as she left the room I heard her say to Cameron, 'You will be *very* careful, Mr. Cameron, will you not?'

I waited, listening for the sound of the front door and for Mr. Cameron's footsteps returning to the office. He was away longer than I expected but when he came back into the room he was still smiling and rubbing his hands.

'Now to take care of you,' he announced briskly. 'There is a room upstairs where you can breakfast and wait till it is time to leave for the Sheriff's office, and no one in the house a penny the wiser – except for my wife, of course. And she, bless her, never troubles her head over any legal bar to providing hospitality!'

His smile broadened at this so that I could not help smiling in reply. The more I saw of Hector Cameron, I decided, the more I liked him, and I followed him from the room feeling suddenly envious of the boy whose clothes I wore.

I was prepared to like Mrs. Cameron also from the moment I saw her smiling at me from the doorway of the upstairs room in which Mr. Cameron had left me. I jumped to my feet as she appeared there with a tray of breakfast in her hands, and hurried to help her with it. I had hardly begun to explain myself, however, and to apologize for my presence in the house before she cut me off with, 'No, no, boy. You are not to tell me your name or why you are here. Then I can say truthfully that I know nothing about you.'

It was said with a smile and she turned at the door to smile again at me before she left, but all the same her words impressed my outcast state so keenly on my mind that I could have echoed Rory Ruadh's bitter cry:

'My name is Ishmael!'

I only picked at the food on the tray, for now that I was alone and had time to think my stomach was churning with sick fear at the prospect of meeting face to face with the man who had been hounding me. There was a clock somewhere near at hand that struck the half and quarter hours, and I kept listening for the sound of it with my heart leaping afresh at each of the

124

sweet chiming peals it rang. Nothing less like the bold creature Mr. Cameron had taken me for could have been imagined, I thought, and rubbed at my sweating palms with a white handkerchief I found in a pocket of the suit that did not belong to me.

The quarter before ten had struck and died away again when Mr. Cameron appeared in the doorway. With a look that said I must follow him and a gesture that commanded silence, he led me through the house and down the stairs to the front door. He closed it quietly behind us saying under his breath, 'Walk a little behind me. And here, take my brief-case. It will look very natural for you to be carrying it for me.'

I took the leather bag he had called a brief-case carefully from him, and followed him up the street. A minute's walk from his house brought us to the High Street. As we turned into it, Cameron glanced back over his shoulder. When he saw how carefully I was carrying the brief-case he muttered, 'Swing that case about, boy – be careless with it! At fifteen a clerk has no respect for his master's property!'

I tried to do as he bade me, but my mind was much more on the faces of the people hurrying past us than on the way a clerk should handle a brief-case. There were people in Tain who knew me – grain merchants, cattle-drovers and the like. The fear of being recognized grew on me to the point that I hardly noticed how close we were to the great stone pile of the Tolbooth. I followed blindly as Mr. Cameron mounted the steps to the front door, and only came to a proper realization of where we were when the bees-wax and pine-panelling smell of its interior closed in on me.

Cameron was walking ahead of me still, his feet beating a measured tread on the stone floor of the passage we had entered. A clerk with a sheaf of paper in his hand brushed past us. A man in the uniform of the constabulary followed the clerk and my brain cried 'Run!' but my feet continued to move mechanically forward. The man in uniform passed without so much as a glance at us. Then Cameron stopped in front of a door with a name picked out in gold lettering on its dark panels. He knocked. A voice called, 'Come in!' I followed him through the door and found myself face to face with Sheriff Taylor.

'Ah, Cameron, ye're early,' he said peevishly, and to me he shouted, 'Well then, close the door, can't you!'

I turned hastily to shut the door and Cameron added, 'And sit down out of the road with your book. Over there.'

He gestured to a side table. I went quickly over to it, and opening the brief-case I fumbled inside it guessing that the pencil and the book for taking notes must be in it.

As he did this the Sheriff said, 'So you're taking notes, eh, Cameron? Well, two can play at that game and I prefer to have my own record.'

He lifted a hand-bell on his desk and rang it, glancing at me as he did so. Cameron sat down facing him.

'Please yourself, Sheriff,' he said blandly. 'It was more for practice in the speed-writing than anything else that I brought the boy with me. These Hansard reporters have to be fast you know, very fast.'

'So it's a Hansard reporter he wants to be.'

The Sheriff's glance at me turned into a stare. 'Interesting,' he commented, and then, 'He's very sun-burned for a city boy and a clerk, Mr. Cameron.'

Cameron laughed. 'You have a shrewd eye, Sheriff. He is neither a city boy nor a clerk!'

I had my head bent over the note-book I had taken out of the brief-case but Cameron's words brought it jerking up in a sickening spasm of fear. Before I could move to speak to betray myself, however, he went on quickly, 'He's the son of a client I have taken under my wing as a favour. As to the sunburn, poor lad, he got that recuperating from an illness in the country.'

I bent my head again, overcome with relief and admiration for Cameron's verbal skill. He had misled the Sheriff

126

completely about me, and had done so – as he had promised would be the case – without telling a single lie! The Sheriff himself only grunted and waved the young man who had come in answer to the bell to sit down opposite me. He did so, with a quick appraising glance at my elegant version of his own thread-bare clerk's clothing, and sat languidly leaning his chin in his hand and staring into space.

'Now to your purpose, Cameron,' the Sheriff said, 'and be brief, man, brief.'

'An instruction after my own heart,' Cameron answered him briskly. 'In a word then, Sheriff, when Anne Ross and Peter Ross of Greenyards come up for trial on the 14th of this month I want all the charges against them – mobbing and rioting and breach of the peace and, against Anne Ross, the charge of attempted murder – to be reduced to a charge of breach of the peace only.'

I scribbled furiously as Cameron spoke, imitating the actions of the clerk sitting opposite me and keeping one hand over my book so that he could not see the sprawls and pothooks I was making. We both looked up in the silence that followed Cameron's speech.

The Sheriff was leaning forward on the arms of his chair, staring at Cameron with his mouth half-open. His lower jaw was working as he tried to find speech and his face had flushed a deep angry red. The veins on his forehead were standing out like cords and even the loose bags of skin under his eyes were puffed out with blood.

'You are pleased to make some sort of joke, Mr. Cameron,' he managed at last. 'But I'll not stomach it! No sir, you shall not so bring the law into disrepute.'

'I am afraid you will have to stomach it, Sheriff,' Cameron interrupted calmly. 'I am instructed otherwise, to bring a charge of murder against you.'

Sheriff Taylor rose to his feet and pushed his chair back. Slowly and distinctly he said :

'Hector Cameron, I think you must have gone clean out of your wits. You are mad, man – utterly mad!'

'Sit down, Sheriff.' Cameron was as composed as ever. 'You will find that the proposition I have to put to you is a perfectly sane one.'

'I'll not listen to you, Cameron, d'you hear me!' With his clenched fist Sheriff Taylor struck angrily at the desk in front of him. 'I'll not listen to you!'

'You will listen – by thunder you will listen!'

Cameron jumped to his feet and snatched the brief-case from in front of my nose. He snapped the catch open, seized a handful of papers from inside the case, and threw them on the Sheriff's desk.

'Look at them!' he commanded. 'Look carefully, Sheriff, and you might find your own death-warrant among them!'

'Eh?' Sheriff Taylor's bloodshot gaze went slowly down to the papers. 'What are you talking about, Cameron? What *are* these?'

'Call them a summary of the evidence that will be brought against you,' Cameron said. 'There is a copy of the death certificate of Ellen McGregor Ross who died shortly after the constables under your command attacked the women of Green-yards. The cause of death, you will see, is given as a violent blow which fractured her skull.

'Beside this certificate you will find a number of affidavits which were lodged in my care by a journalist called Donald Ross. These affidavits were obtained from the women who witnessed the blow that killed Ellen MacGregor Ross. They testify to the blow being struck by one of your constables, and also that it followed your command to *"Knock them down"* – "them" being the women of whom Ellen MacGregor Ross was one.'

He paused. Sheriff Taylor sat down. 'I see,' he said. He pulled the papers towards him and drummed thoughtfully on them with his finger-tips. 'Go on, Cameron, go on.'

Cameron sat down again also. 'With pleasure,' he said. 'I told you what I wanted at the beginning of this interview. Do as I ask and my clients will not press this charge against you. That is the bargain I have to propose to you.'

'For a lawyer, Cameron, you talk a deal of rubbish,' Sheriff Taylor retorted. 'You know as well as I do that neither I nor anyone else has the power to stop these charges being brought against the prisoners in court now that they have actually been filed against them. All that can be done is to wait for the trial and then ask the Advocate Depute to accept a plea in answer to the minor charge of breach of the peace only. And it is certainly not within *my* power to convince him he should do so!'

'Take it from me that you will find the Advocate Depute willing to do as I ask once he learns the consequence of refusal,' Cameron told him blandly. 'His part in the trial of Anne Ross and Peter Ross would inevitably involve him in a prosecution against you, after all, and I do not think a law-officer of his rank will care to have his career placed at risk by being involved in such an unsavoury proceeding.'

'You have considered the Procurator Fiscal too, no doubt,' the Sheriff sneered. 'It is *his* function to compile the evidence for the precognition on which these charges are based, remember – not mine!'

'Who supplied that evidence to the Fiscal in the first place?' Cameron asked. 'And when you have answered that question, Sheriff, remind yourself that the Fiscal was himself present at the murder of Ellen MacGregor Ross. A charge against you would therefore involve him also. He might even find himself being cited by my clients as having been "art and part" in the crime since he made no protest when you ordered the attack on the women – a possibility he will be quick to realize for himself when you inform him of our conversation.'

'You could never prove such a charge!' the Sheriff retorted. 'Why, this journalist fellow who went prowling like a hyena

129

round Greenyards after the event actually published a pamphlet accusing me of all sorts of atrocities. And what happened? Nothing! Precisely nothing! Some people read it, no doubt, and a few sentimentalists held up their hands in horror, but nothing was done, my dear fellow. Nothing was done because no one believed the rubbish in it any more than a judge or jury would. No, you cannot prove it, and there's an end of it!'

'For my purposes,' Cameron said, 'it will not be necessary to *prove* the charge of murder against you. The scandal of its being brought will be enough to ruin you, Sheriff. It is one thing, after all, for these charges to be made in a pamphlet hawked about the streets, and quite another for them to be made in due legal order in the High Court of Justiciary. And I use the word "scandal" advisedly, sir, for your trial would not take place in some obscure Circuit Court like that of Anne Ross. Oh, no! As an officer of the Crown you would have to face the charge of murder in the High Court in Edinburgh – the capital, my dear Sheriff, not only of the country's serious affairs but of its news and views – and especially of its gossip!'

He paused and looked steadily at Sheriff Taylor. 'It would break you, Sheriff. Even if you were acquitted, the scandal of the attack on the women of Greenyards would break you. There would be questions asked in Parliament, inquiries made about the dead woman. The land-owners of Ross-shire would take alarm at such a public light on their affairs and bring pressure on you to resign your office. You would —'

'If you are sure of this,' Sheriff Taylor interrupted, 'why do you ask only for a reduction of the charges against Anne Ross? Why not use all the weight of this supposed evidence against me to try and secure an acquittal for her?'

'For the simple and very good reason that the jury at this Circuit Court, as you well know, will consist of local land-owners and their hangers-on, and no such jury would go against their own interests by acquitting her and condemning you – whatever the evidence! I would lose my case for her and if I took the matter to the High Court in Edinburgh I might still lose my case against you. The scandal of such a proceeding would still break you, of course, but Anne Ross would be no better off for that! No, Sheriff, much as it grieves me I have to admit that this compromise on the charges is the best – the only bargain I can make for my client in the present circumstances.'

Abruptly the Sheriff asked, 'How would she plead to the lesser charge?'

'Guilty,' Cameron told him. 'They would both plead guilty. So you would obtain the conviction you need – a minor one certainly, but still enough to keep your position secure, and all fear of scandal would be buried for ever. Think of that, Sheriff!'

Sheriff Taylor rose to his feet and walked over to the window. He stood there with his back to us and his hands clasped under his coat-tails, while his clerk and Cameron and myself all watched him intently. There was no sound in the room but a faint spluttering from the logs burning in the fireplace behind the Sheriff's desk, and so it continued till he asked, still looking out of the window:

'Who *are* you acting for in this, Cameron? Some of the Greenyards rioters?'

He looked sharply over his shoulder at the lawyer. 'I warn you, they are a bankrupt crew! You will not even get your fee out of them, much less the expenses of a High Court action against me.'

'My clients' identity is my own affair,' Cameron told him. 'But as to money, I can tell you that there was a sum to cover Anne Ross's legal expenses deposited with me only three days after she was arrested.'

That was also perfectly true, I thought, but still totally misleading, of course. Sheriff Taylor weighed the information, his eyes boring at the back of Cameron's head.

Then, 'You are bluffing, Cameron,' he said. 'You are just trying to panic me with this cock-and-bull yarn of a counter-prosecution.'

Cameron did not turn round. 'That, Sheriff,' he said to the ceiling, 'is your privilege to decide.'

Sheriff Taylor snorted and turned back to the window. There was another silence and then he burst out:

'Hang it, Cameron, you know I can do nothing without the agreement of the Fiscal and the Advocate Depute!'

He turned round and came to stand over Cameron's chair. 'You will have to give me time to talk it over with them. D'you understand? I need time, man, before I can come to any sort of decision over this.'

'They will agree to my bargain if you put it to them as I have put it to you,' Cameron told him calmly.

He rose and stood face to face with Sheriff Taylor. 'Decide now, Sheriff. But be warned that if you do not take my bargain I will accuse you to the Lord Advocate this very day.'

'This is blackmail, Cameron.' Sheriff Taylor's voice shook on the words. 'Blackmail!' he repeated.

But Cameron only answered with another, 'Decide, Sheriff, decide!'

I held my breath as the two men stared eye to eye at one another. The clerk beside me was staring also, his mouth open and all his former pretence of indifference vanished in the tension of the moment.

Sheriff Taylor was the first to break away from that inter-locking stare. He sighed suddenly, spread out his hands and said, 'You are devilish hard on an old man, Cameron. You know I could not afford to ride out such a storm at this late stage in my career.'

'Decide then, Sheriff,' Cameron repeated inexorably.

'Very well.' Sullen, his shoulders drooping with defeat, the Sheriff turned away from the lawyer. 'I will persuade the

132

Advocate Depute to accept the plea of "Guilty" to breach of the peace only.'

'And I, in my turn,' said Cameron, 'will post you this evidence on the day that the two prisoners leave the country, as they intend to do as soon as they are set free. Until then it must remain their safeguard against possible further action by you.'

'How do I know you will not use it against me before then?' the Sheriff demanded.

'You will have to take my word for that – as I am having to take yours that you will keep your part of the bargain.'

Cameron had been gathering the affidavits together again as he spoke, but now he looked up from them and with a taunting inflexion in his voice he added, 'Unless, that is, you care to put our agreement in writing.'

'No, no, nothing in writing!' the Sheriff said hastily. 'These notes, also – they must be destroyed.'

Advancing on me with the words he held out his hand for the notes his clerk had taken and for mine also. Obediently the clerk handed over his book, and it did not need the warning glance Cameron shot at me to tell me how close we would be to discovery if the Sheriff saw the meaningless scrawls I had made. I rose quickly ignoring the Sheriff's outstretched hand, crossed over to the fire behind his desk and dropped my book into the flames.

'There you are!' Cameron exclaimed in a loud jovial voice that sounded painfully false to me. 'There is a complete end to my clerk's knowledge of the interview, Sheriff. And you need have no fear that he can make use of anything he has remembered, for he is leaving Tain soon – leaving Scotland altogether, in fact.'

Once again it was the truth in boldly misleading form, but still I kept my face bent to the fire and poked at the logs till the Sheriff said impatiently:

'Yes, yes, I know. A cub Hansard reporter on his way to London, you said. I remember.'

I straightened up, relief flooding over me. 'As for you,' the Sheriff was saying to his own clerk, 'you know better than to open your mouth about this. Be off with you!'

The clerk flushed and went deathly pale again at the grinding menace in the Sheriff's voice. He scuttled from the room with a single terrified glance backwards as he closed the door. Cameron moved over to the table, picked up his brief-case and pushed the affidavits into it.

'Here you are, boy.' He crossed to hand the case to me. I took it from him and moved ahead of him to the door.

'Good day to you, Sheriff.' Cameron turned at the door and bowed. 'I look forward to our meeting in court on the 14th.'

I was out of the door before he had finished speaking. He caught me up half-way along the corridor, grasped my shoulder and hissed, 'Slow down, you fool! Walk naturally.'

I slowed my pace with a great effort of will. Cameron took the lead from me and like this we walked out of the front door of the Tolbooth. I saw McCaig standing there on the steps a fraction before Cameron turned a startled face to warn me of his presence, and without any conscious planning on my own part I jerked the brief-case forward out of my hand so that it bounced down the steps and on to the pavement below.

I ran after it, keeping Cameron between myself and McCaig, and bent to pick it up. Cameron was on me before I rose and fetched me a stinging slap on either side of the face. With a roar of pain that was not entirely pretended I turned away from him, bent double with my face hidden between my hands. Cameron followed me, aiming further blows at my head and swearing loudly at my supposed clumsiness with his brief-case. McCaig's laughter followed us down the street, and for once it was a sweet sound in my ears.

'Quick thinking, boy,' Cameron complimented me as I

straightened up again. There was a turn of the High Street between us and the Tolbooth now, but he glanced back all the same to see if McCaig was following. 'No sign of the fellow,' he told me. 'You fooled him there, Connal!'

I grinned back at him. 'We fooled him between us. You are very quick to pick up a move, Mr. Cameron.'

'That's what training in the law does for you, and I am a very good lawyer,' Cameron boasted. 'Could you not see that from the way I twisted the Sheriff's tail?'

'You drove him hard,' I admitted.

'I had him cornered,' Cameron said complacently. 'All we have to fear now is the sentence Lord Justice Clerk Hope will impose. He is a harsh man, you understand – but even so, breach of the peace is a simple misdemeanour which does not normally carry a heavy penalty.'

He glanced at me smilingly as we walked along, but when he saw no answering smile on my face, his look changed. After a minute he said, 'So you are still not convinced there is no need for that pistol of yours in court?'

I found it hard to meet the serious, expectant look he turned on me. I knew nothing of the law and the argument in the Sheriff's office had seemed a very complicated affair to me. It had been only too easy, however, to appreciate the menace in the Sheriff's *You're bluffing!* I could not forget the uneasiness I had felt then, and I was miserably aware how fast the doubts of Cameron's plan were breeding again in my mind.

I summoned all my slipping courage and met his eyes frankly. 'I am sorry, sir. I am not truly convinced your plan will succeed.'

I do not know what I expected of him – anger, or disappointment, or perhaps another plea for me to see matters his way. Certainly I did not expect him to shrug his shoulders and say casually, 'Well, boy, *I* am convinced the Sheriff will keep his bargain and so it makes no difference whether or not you carry the pistol into court. You will never need to fire it.'

I said nothing to this for my mind had flashed back to a thought which had occurred to me during the few minutes I had been alone in Cameron's office that morning. We continued to walk along together in silence till Cameron turned up a little side-street and stopped in front of one of a row of tall, narrow houses.

'Mistress McKay's lodging-house,' he said, and knocked at the door.

As we waited for it to open he said, 'The emigrant ship, *Good Chance*, sails from the port of Fort William for the Americas on the 21st of this month, Connal, and the shipping agent in Tain tells me there are still a few passages to be had aboard her. If you and your sister are prepared to leave on that ship after the trial you will find yourself in the company of many of the Greenyards people.'

'I thought they would all have been gone long since!' I said, astonished.

Cameron turned a bleak face on me. 'These ships do not sail to any schedule,' he told me grimly. 'They lie in port for months gathering as many passengers as the master thinks the vessel will hold without foundering. Therein lies his profit and, in this case, the reason for the delayed departure of your friends.'

The door opened before I could answer him. I had a quick glimpse of a grey-haired plump woman and a flight of steps behind her with Katrine standing at the top of them. My mind flew back immediately to the thought that had been interrupted by the talk of emigrant ships, and briefly excusing myself I brushed past the grey-haired woman and ran up the stairs. Katrine retreated before me towards a door at the top of the stairs. She opened it and went ahead of me into the room beyond.

It was a small room with little more than a narrow, white-covered bed in it. My pistol lay on the bed, a black, ugly stroke on the whiteness. I snatched it up and took it over to the light of the window in the opposite wall.

'If you have tampered with it . . .' I threw the unfinished threat over my shoulder at Katrine.

'Why should I?' she demanded.

'Cameron was a long time seeing you to the door of his house this morning, and he was very casual just now when I said I still intended to take the pistol into court with me. Why was that, eh? Did he tell you this morning to tamper with it while I was at the Sheriff's office with him – to do something to it so that it would not fire?'

All the time I was talking I was examining the pistol, unloading it, checking the powder, the ball and wad, and trying the firing action. There was nothing wrong with any of them but I was taking no chances and so I carefully reloaded with a fresh charge of powder. Satisfied then, and feeling slightly ashamed of my suspicions, I looked up at Katrine.

'You see,' she said coldly, 'it was exactly as you left it.'

'Yes,' I admitted. 'I am sorry I doubted you, Katrine.'

Turning from her I raised the pistol, and training it on an imaginary figure of McCaig, I said exultantly, 'One shot, and I shall have him!'

'There is still time enough before the trial for even you to see reason,' Katrine told me tartly.

'I saw plenty of reason when Cameron was arguing with the Sheriff this morning,' I retorted, 'but now that I think back on it, it all sounded like so much legal trickery to me. I do not trust tricks, Katrine – especially when the Sheriff is playing the same game, and so I mean to be ready in my own way whatever you say.'

She sighed and came over to stand beside me at the window. 'I wonder what it will be like at the trial,' she said after a moment. 'I wonder, Conn. I wonder.'

So did I. I wondered a great deal.

We had another four days and the long coach journey into
Inverness on the day of the trial for our fears and curiosity to
grow, and it seemed to me that this time would never pass. But
somehow it did and the morning of the 14th of September
found Katrine, Cameron and myself a part of the steady trickle
of people climbing the steep hill of Castle Wynd towards the
Castle of Inverness.

We took our leave of Cameron just inside the great iron-
bossed door of the castle. Katrine's arm was linked in mine
and I could feel it trembling as we climbed the stairs to the
gallery of the court-room.

'Bear up, Katrine. We look no different from any of those
others,' I whispered to reassure her. And indeed it was true,
for Katrine was as neat and pretty as any young woman there,
and in my borrowed clothes I looked as elegant and responsible
as any of the young men squiring them.

It wanted a quarter to ten o'clock when we came through the
narrow door at the top of the gallery stairs, and the court-room
below us was filling up rapidly with spectators and officials.
The gallery itself was more than half-full already, but there was

still time enough for me to secure the position I wanted in the semi-circular rows of seats. I led Katrine to the right-hand end of the curve where there were two vacant seats in the front row. It had to be the front row, I had decided, if I were to get a clear shot at McCaig. I seated her beside me and gazed curiously around the court-room below us.

It was all as Cameron had sketched it in his office for us, from the Judge's tall chair of red leather to the dock in the centre of the court. I scanned it quickly and turned to examine the faces of the robed and wigged figures at the solicitors' table. The Advocate Depute would be sitting at its right-hand side, according to Cameron. I picked him out from the others there and studied him carefully.

It was a dark, narrow face I saw, thin-nosed, with a heavy bar of eyebrows which looked very black against the whiteness of his wig. Shrewd, watchful eyes flickered under the heavy brows.

It was the face of a clever man, I decided. The face of a man young for the position he held and so likely to have ambitions towards an even higher one. And I wondered just how far the risk of being involved in the scandal of a murder-plea against Sheriff Taylor would deter an ambitious man from pushing the prosecution's case against my mother.

The seats on either side of the Judge's chair were filling up now. Town Councillors in scarlet and ermine were filing solemnly through a red-curtained doorway towards the seats on the right of the chair, and through a similar doorway on the left came Sheriffs, Sheriff-Officers and other representatives of the law. I was searching eagerly amongst these men for a sight of McCaig when a fanfare of trumpets drew my attention back to the opposite side of the court-room.

I turned to see the red and blue figures of two trumpeters stationed in front of the red curtain on that side. The silver trumpets sounded again and everyone rose to their feet. The curtain parted. A tall, thin figure, red-robed and white-wigged, swept through. It paused in front of the Judge's chair and like a thin, immense puppet bowed stiffly to the Court. Katrine's hand in the small of my back pushed me forward to bow in return as everyone else was doing. The tall red figure bent in another bow. It seated itself in the chair. A rustling sound as the Court seated itself again, a slow raising of the white-wigged head, and I saw at last the face of Lord Justice Clerk Hope, the man who would preside over my mother's trial.

It was white as tallow, white as the deep collar of white fur laid over his shoulders, with a thin, purplish gash of mouth under the crooked great beak of his nose. Pale eyes as dull as the eyes of a dead fish looked slowly down into the well of the court-room and as slowly up to the gallery. I shivered at the sight of them, and glancing away from the inhuman coldness of their stare, found myself looking straight at Dugald McCaig.

He was seated beside Sheriff Taylor in the part of the court-room reserved for law-officers, and as my eyes came to rest on his heavy, whiskered face I felt hatred turn like a knife inside me. I leaned forward with my left elbow resting on my knee and my hand to my brow to mask my face. The pistol under my coat pressed hard into my side with the movement. I mentally gauged the distance between myself and McCaig and made it about twenty-five feet.

There was no chance that I would miss him at that range, no chance either that the pistol would misfire, for it had not been out of my possession since I had checked and reloaded it that day on my return from the Sheriff's office. I could not miss – I *would* not miss, I vowed, and settled down to wait for my mother's case to be called.

It was third on the list of business for that day. I looked up several times under my hand before the usher's voice calling her name went echoing through the court-room, and on two of these occasions I saw McCaig's eyes wandering over the people in the public benches below us and then glancing up towards the gallery. Each time his gaze stopped short of where I sat, for as Cameron had indicated would be the case, our seats were out of the immediate range of his vision. Despite this safeguard, however, I was still cautious enough to keep my face hidden behind the screen of my hand. It was only when I saw my mother in the little line of prisoners and warders shuffling forward to take her place beside Peter Ross in the dock that I sat upright, forgetting the need for caution in my rage at what had been done to her.

She had aged ten years since I last saw her. Her shoulders were bowed like those of an old woman and her dark hair was streaked with grey, but much worse than that was the great purple-red scar that split one side of her face jaggedly from cheek-bone to chin.

It was a horrible thing, the gaping lips of it all puckered and twisted on either side of the livid line of the wound. The sight of it drew a murmur from the public benches, and a slow, painful stain of scarlet spread over my mother's face at the sound. Her head drooped. I saw Peter Ross bend down and whisper to her, then straighten up with one hand laid encouragingly on her shoulder. She raised her head again. The flush on her face had died away, leaving the scar standing out even more cruelly than before. She kept her head high, all the same, and it was all I could do not to jump up and shout aloud my gratitude to Peter Ross and my pride in the courage it took for her to stand so.

The Clerk of the Court began to read out the charges. There was a long list of them, and the complicated legal way in which they were phrased seemed to swell their enormity. As the Clerk's toneless voice rattled out one accusation after another, Greenyards and all that it stood for began to seem very far away to me. The formal setting of the Court closed suddenly in around me with a new and alarming significance so that I felt a sweat of fear spring out on my brow when the Clerk said,

'. . . *and the said Anne Ross did then cause a loaded fire-arm to be presented at Sheriff-Officer McCaig with intent to discharge the same with danger to his life. And did thereby assault and attempt the life of a Sheriff-Officer in the execution of his duty . . .'*

This was the crucial charge. I slid my hand inside my coat to rest on the butt of the pistol and glanced quickly at the boyish-looking face of Moncrieff, our Counsel, and from there to the dark, clever face of the Advocate Depute. I could read nothing from either of them. Moncrieff looked bored. The Advocate Depute was impassive. The Clerk's voice rattled on through the final charge of mobbing and rioting on the 31st of March – the day of the Sheriff's assault on us. A pause, and a dry crackling of papers from around the solicitors' table, and then the Clerk asked:

'How do you plead – Guilty, or Not Guilty?'

Moncrieff rose to his feet. 'My lord, my clients desire to enter a plea of guilty to breach of the peace only.'

He sat down again. The tallow-white face of the Judge swung slowly from him to the Advocate Depute. In the pause while the Advocate Depute rose slowly to his feet I closed my grip firmly round the butt of the pistol. If Moncrieff's plea was refused – if the Advocate Depute insisted on pushing the full charges against my mother, it would mean that the Sheriff had failed to keep his bargain. Whether by design or through circumstances beyond his control would not be clear till later but the reason for it would make no difference to me. I had to stop McCaig bringing his twisted evidence against my mother, I had to convince the Court of my own guilt, and that meant I would have to draw and shoot immediately.

The Advocate Depute spoke quietly. 'My lord, the Crown accepts the plea to the reduced charge of breach of the peace.'

A buzz of whispering broke out from the spectators. The Judge's harsh voice rasped through the sound.

'You are certain you are making a correct decision, Mr. Fordyce?'

'Perfectly, my lord.' The dark, clever face remained impassive in spite of the disapproval in the Judge's voice. 'The Crown considers that the evidence in the Procurator Fiscal's precognition is not sufficient to support the other charges.'

Moncrieff was on his feet immediately. 'My lord, since the Advocate Depute accept my clients' plea, I move for sentence on the charge of breach of the peace.'

The bloodless mask of the Judge's face turned slowly back towards him. 'I do not accept your move, Mr. Moncrieff,' the rasping voice told him, 'and I will thank you, therefore, to sit down.'

Moncrieff threw a bewildered glance at Cameron but he sat down, nevertheless. The Judge looked past him to the figures of Peter Ross and my mother in the dock, and went on speaking to them.

'It would appear that some technical aspect of evidence prevents the prosecution from demanding for you that punishment which you so richly deserve – a state of affairs both deplorable and unsatisfactory in view of the spirit of unrest against the law of property presently abroad in this land. However, you are not to be allowed to suppose you can continue in the wicked and rebellious spirit you have displayed, and to that end, and in order to give myself time to consider the action appropriate to your case, I propose to defer passing sentence on you until the end of this Court's sitting.'

I turned briefly in astonishment and dismay to Katrine and found her leaning, white-faced, towards me.

'McCaig is watching us,' she whispered.

I glanced downwards and fear crept suddenly cold over the

back of my neck as I saw McCaig half-turned in his seat and seeming to look straight up at me.

So much for my caution at the beginning of the Court's sitting! He could have been watching me all the time my mother was in the dock for all I knew, for I had been too carried away by what was happening in the court-room to remember about keeping my face hidden.

Quickly I bent forward to lean my head in my hand again, cursing the folly that had allowed him to see me. And all for nothing, too! Let the Judge disapprove and frown as he might now, the attempted murder charge had still been dropped by the Advocate Depute. Cameron's plan *had* succeeded, and so there was no longer any point in my own plan.

It was worse than pointless now, I thought, dismayed. It had become a trap for myself. With the delay the Judge had ordered I was pinned there under McCaig's eyes until the end of the hearings for that day. I could only leave the gallery before then at the risk of drawing more attention to myself – perhaps even confirming, by such a move, whatever guess he had made at my identity.

I shot a glance under my hand at McCaig. He was still looking up towards me, and for a wild moment I was tempted to draw my pistol and make a bolt for the gallery door. With the pistol as a threat to clear my path I might be down the gallery steps before McCaig could get clear of the court-room, and in that case, I reasoned, I would have a good chance of escaping altogether from the castle.

The knowledge that failure and capture in such circumstances would only further influence the Judge against my mother made me fight down the temptation. Besides, I argued to myself, it was still not completely certain that McCaig had recognized me. The minutes were passing and he had made no move except to throw occasional glances in our direction again. I kept my eyes on him and tried to empty my mind of all arguments. All I could do now was to watch and wait and be ready for whatever trouble might arise.

The case in hand came to an end and the next case – the last one of the day – was called. McCaig's eyes were still wandering in my direction. The court-room seemed full of voices to me – loud voices, persuasive voices, frightened voices, the rasping voice of the Judge. McCaig's eyes were resting longer on us and at more frequent intervals. I had to fight so hard now to control my impulse to jump up and run that, in the end, I missed the re-call of my mother and Peter Ross to the dock.

A sharp dig in the ribs from Katrine brought me back to the business in hand. Peter Ross and my mother were standing together in the dock and Moncrieff had launched out into a plea of leniency for them. He spoke well, better than I would have given him credit for. I watched the Judge's face for a sign that he was affected by our Counsel's speech but he remained expressionless to the end.

'A harsh man,' Cameron had called him and I had already seen for myself that there was no spark of mercy in that death's head of a face. Yet somehow, even as I had sweated coldly with the fear of McCaig's eyes on me, I had still hoped the postponing of sentence had only been a petty display of power on the Judge's part.

Now I knew differently, for as soon as his harsh voice began once again to lecture my mother and Peter Ross on the wickedness and folly of their resistance to the Law of Property, it became very clear that Lord Justice Clerk Hope meant to lay on them the heaviest sentence that lay within his power.

I clenched my hands together in a fierce effort of self-control as the merciless voice rasped on and on. Beside me I felt Katrine trembling as if she had a fever. Tears dripped on to her lap and I reached out my hand to her as the Judge began to pronounce:

'I therefore sentence Peter Ross to eighteen months in prison with hard labour, and Anne Ross to twelve months.'

A gasping sound like the breaking of a wave on the shore went up from the spectators at the severity of the sentence. I had a sudden flashing glimpse of Cameron's face turning wide-eyed with shock towards my mother swaying against Peter Ross in the dock, then Katrine slumped against me. I caught her and held her upright in her seat, only dimly aware through my own shock of the Judge's formal speech of thanks to the jury before the silver trumpets announced his departure from the court-room.

I had to get Katrine out of the place. I had to find Cameron – see my mother – get away from McCaig's probing eyes. But the gallery doorway was blocked now with people trying to get out. Desperately I looked for help and, ironically, it was the Law that came to my aid. The constable on duty at the door caught my eye and cleared a way for us calling:

'Gangway! Gangway there! Young lady's fainting!'

Half-pulling, half-carrying Katrine, I got her through the door and blundered down the stairs with her. There was a bench a little way along the broad marble passage at the foot of the stairs. She revived within seconds of my setting her down on it, and said immediately:

'We must see her, Connal. We *must* see her!'

'We will have to find Cameron,' I said. 'See if you can walk.'

I made to help her up again and from the corner of my eye saw McCaig turn towards us out of a passage that could only have led from the court-room. He was not more than five yards away from us. The only exit from the castle visible to me and the only one I knew of was the door through which we had entered, and it was still blocked by spectators leaving the court. There was nothing I could do but bluff my way out of the trap.

All this went through my mind at such lightning speed that there was scarcely a pause between my sighting McCaig and

146

taking avoiding action. I put one foot up on the bench beside Katrine and bent towards her so that my face was turned away from McCaig. I had no scruples now about using the ruse she had suggested to me in Tain. I leaned over her like a lover, holding one of her hands clasped between my own. As I gazed into her eyes, McCaig's footsteps passed behind me. He was walking very slowly. I sensed his eyes on the back of my head and the goose-flesh rose up on my skin. The slow footsteps passed us and went on, slower still, in the direction of the castle door. I smiled fondly down at Katrine and whispered,

'Is he looking back?'

'Yes.' She simpered at me. 'He has stopped. He is staring back at you.'

'Wait here, Katrine. If McCaig follows me, find Cameron.'

I stretched a last, lingering smile from my unwilling features, dropped my foot from the bench, and made the few swift strides that took me to the turn of the passage. Once round it, I ran.

Ahead of me on my right was the circular wall of the court-room. A passage forked diagonally away from it on my left. It was empty. I ran along it, hesitated for a moment at the first door I came to, and listened. There was no sound from inside, and assuming an empty room on the other side of the door, I turned the handle. As I pushed the door open McCaig came round the corner of the passage. I stepped swiftly through the door, closed it behind me, and turned to find myself face to face with a constable seated behind a small table. I froze where I stood, paralysed by the shock of the moment. The constable rose menacingly to his feet.

'You are not allowed in here!' he snorted. 'This is the library – private to the legal gentlemen!'

My brain began working again on the instant. I was in a small ante-room, I realized, and the door on the constable's left must lead into the library he had mentioned. Calmly I said:

'I have a message for Mr. Cameron of Tain, constable,' and was at the door in two strides as I spoke.

The constable was slow-witted. I had the door open before he had framed any objection to my move. McCaig was still hard on my heels, however, for the door into the ante-room opened as I stepped through the door into the library. Yet still my luck held. I stepped straight into Cameron swinging round from a table with a bundle of books in his hands.

'McCaig!' I blurted. 'Out there – he's after me!'

Cameron took in my meaning so quickly that his movement from the table to the door was almost continuous. He thrust the books into my hands as he passed me and I was still looking stupidly at them when I heard, first his voice, and then Mc-Caig's coming from the ante-room. The voices rose and cut across one another in argument, McCaig's angry, Cameron's sharp and contemptuous. I strained my ears to hear them through the buzz of conversation from little groups of 'legal gentlemen' standing about in the library.

'You are making a fool of yourself again, you drunken lout!' I heard Cameron say. 'The boy was simply one of my clerks who offered to take care of the girl at the trial.'

An angry mutter from McCaig followed by a laugh from Cameron came after this, then the door of the library opened and Cameron reappeared. He looked me up and down and said sourly:

'I was forced into telling a lie there on your behalf.'

I put the books on the table. 'Has he gone?'

'Yes, but not for good, I imagine. That man is stupid, but he suspects you and he has a nose like a bloodhound for a fugitive.'

'My mother —?' I asked. 'Can we see her now?'

'Wait here,' Cameron said. He went outside and a moment later reappeared again. 'I am saved the trouble of fetching your sister,' he said. 'She followed McCaig here.'

I went through the ante-room with him into the passage and

found Katrine waiting there for us. Cameron pushed us ahead of him with a brusque: 'Straight ahead to the door at the farther end.'

We hurried along to the door at the far end of the passage. The constable on duty outside it snapped to attention as we neared him, and at Cameron's command unlocked the door. Katrine and I passed through it and into our mother's cell.

She did not speak at first and neither did we, but it was not from lack of feeling in any of us for I am not ashamed to confess that I wept as freely then as Katrine and herself.

'You have not written to tell your father anything of this?' she asked anxiously when we had all recovered ourselves a little.

We shook our heads and with a sigh of relief she said, 'There's my good bairns! I am not wanting him to learn anything of this trouble sooner than he must.'

'The sentence, ma'am,' I asked. 'Will he not be home before the year of it is up?'

'No,' she said. 'Mr. Cameron has heard that his regiment is under orders to go to the Crimea. It will be a long time, I doubt, before he has home leave again.'

She looked at us, trying to smile. 'And by that time, my bairns, you will both be settled in a fine new life in the Americas.'

'We'll not go without you!' Katrine cried, but she said sharply, 'Nonsense, girl! Do you think I do not know Connal is pursued. You *must* go!'

'She has the heart of the matter there,' Cameron's voice said behind us. As we turned to him he went on, 'McCaig is hanging about at the foot of Castle Wynd, watching everyone who comes down the brae from the castle. The messenger I sent to bring my carriage from the stables saw him there.'

My mother rose to her feet. She caught Katrine to her and

149

kissed her. Katrine burst out weeping afresh, but Cameron patted her shoulder and said soothingly:

'Bear up, girl. The sentence was a deal stiffer than anyone except that devil of a judge would have dealt out, but a year will soon pass for all of you. And your mother's passage-money to the Americas is safe with me. Rory Ruadh's money will cover it.'

My mother looked steadily at me as he took Katrine's arm and led her gently away. I moved to her. I had grown during my time on the mountain, and now I was some inches taller than she, yet still I could have wept to leave her so. She looked up at me as I laid my hands on her shoulders, and in a voice that trembled she said:

'I could wish that you did not have to remember me so.'

She turned the cheek with the scar on it away from me. I turned her face gently to me again, and bending down, I kissed the scar. The tears came from her eyes at that, but she was smiling at the same time. And so I left her, smiling and weeping together, with her eyes following me to the door and one hand fluttering up to touch the scar I had kissed.

Cameron's carriage was waiting outside the castle door. We bundled into it, with Katrine sitting beside Cameron, and myself on the seat facing them. As it rattled off down the cobbles of Castle Wynd Cameron said, 'Lie down full length on that seat, boy, in case McCaig is still watching out for you leaving the castle.'

I slid down to lie along the seat. Katrine looked towards Bridge Street from one window, Cameron covered the High Street and Church Street from the other, and as the coach turned sharp left from the foot of Castle Wynd into Bridge Street he exclaimed, 'Keep well down! McCaig is watching from the doorway of the wine-shop on the corner of Church Street!'

I lay with my ear pressed to the leather of the seat. The rattle of the coach's wheels down Bridge Street changed to a hollow rumble as it crossed the bridge over the River Ness. Cameron poked his head out of the window at the moment the coach swung to the right to take the Tain road.

'McCaig was standing out in the middle of the road to watch the direction we took,' he said, drawing his head in again.

I straightened up, my left ear still ringing with the sound of the carriage wheels. Nothing further was said and we continued to sit in silence while the coach bumped on mile after mile along the road. Once or twice Cameron frowned and muttered to himself but he did not speak again until, by my reckoning, we were not far off the town of Beauly. Then he turned to Katrine and asked:

'Miss Ross, do you have the money with you to pay for a passage to the Americas for Connal and yourself?'

'Yes, I have it here, sewn into the pocket of my gown,' she told him. 'I have never dared to be without it since we left the cave on the Bodach Mhor.'

Cameron sighed with relief. 'Good girl! Good. Then you can leave straight away to join that ship I told Connal was lying at Fort William.'

'Tonight?' I asked, and Katrine said, 'But Mr. Cameron, we have nothing apart from the passage-money except the clothes we stand up in – and Connal's suit does not even belong to him!'

Cameron flapped impatiently for silence. 'Keep the clothes,' he told me. 'You *must* leave tonight if my reading of McCaig is correct and —'

'But supposing he did manage to arrest me,' I interrupted. 'Could the Sheriff still bring that charge of attempted murder against me after what happened in my mother's case?'

Now that the immediate danger from McCaig was over I had begun to feel ashamed of the fear he had inspired in me and resentful of the way I had been made to run. Cameron looked me over deliberately as I challenged him and said flatly,

'He could, and he would. The case against you would be clear-cut and separate from such charges as were brought against your mother, for your tussle with McCaig took place *before* the day of the attack on the women. All the witnesses you could call in your defence are scattered. The Court would only have your word against McCaig's that he drew first, and they would take his word.'

'You could threaten the Sheriff as you did in my mother's case,' I protested.

Cameron gave a grim little laugh. 'I could,' he acknowledged, 'but I would be wasting my breath. Such tricks work but once, boy, and I only succeeded in your mother's case because I left the Sheriff with no time to think up a counter-move. As he could, believe me! Sheriff Taylor is a shrewd lawyer.'

I needed no further convincing though Katrine apparently still had objections to make. She opened her mouth to argue with Cameron but he carried on ruthlessly over her protests: 'So, we have established that Connal is still in danger of arrest and we know that McCaig suspects he is with us in this carriage. McCaig also knows we have taken the Tain road. Therefore, if he pursues his search for Connal, it is to Tain he will certainly go first.'

He leaned forward, bringing us both towards him with a gesture. 'Now, Tain lies north and east of Inverness, whereas Fort William lies roughly the same distance south-west. And though McCaig thinks you are on your way to Tain, you can deceive him by leaving the coach at Beauly and doubling back southwards through these hills on the left of us, by the Glen Convinth Pass. That will bring you out at Drumnadrochit, on the shores of Loch Ness, and all you will have to do after that is to follow the Great Glen south-west to Fort William where your ship lies waiting for you.'

There was nothing else we could do now except emigrate, I thought, and certainly Cameron's suggestion was a good way of throwing McCaig off our track till the ship sailed. Katrine appeared to have overcome her objections to such a sudden departure for she echoed my thought in words and began to thank Cameron for the way he had helped us.

'I want no thanks, lassie,' he told her. 'I only did my duty by you as a lawyer and a Christian.' He turned to me. 'As for you, Connal, all I want from you is that pistol before you get yourself or your sister into more trouble with it. Give it to me now.'

'No!' I drew back from him holding my hand protectively over the pistol.

The need I had meant it to fulfil had not arisen that day – but there would be other occasions for its use. And besides, it had become more than a weapon to me since that first night I had lain in the cave, watching it gleaming in the firelight. The brave defiance that had reached out from the past to touch me then had made the pistol the symbol of my own defiance, and so long as it remained with me I could feel I was still carrying on the fight against the forces which had driven us from the glen. To give the pistol up would be like giving a token of my surrender to these forces – but how could I explain all this to Cameron?

I looked away from him, casting around in my mind for something that would soften the incivility of my refusal, and I thought of McCaig.

'I may need it to resist McCaig if we fail to throw him off our track,' I pointed out.

'Connal, has this trial taught you nothing?' Cameron leaned earnestly towards me. 'All you can do now is to run from McCaig. You cannot resist him, boy. He represents the Law, and you have just seen how cruelly the Law deals with those who go against it. Be sensible and give me the pistol.'

Stubbornly I shook my head. Cameron sighed. 'You think I do not understand what that weapon means to you,' he said, 'but I do, and I have tried to save your pride because of that. However, if you will not listen to reason —'

His right hand shot out, flipped my coat open and jerked the pistol from my belt. The motion was too quick for me to forestall, but with a shout of anger I lunged at him. He fended me off with his other hand, shouting, 'Watch this, boy! Watch!'

And pointing the pistol at the seat of the carriage, he pulled the trigger.

It clicked forward. Nothing happened – there was no report! Cameron clicked the trigger again – and again. Still the gun did not fire. I sank back on my seat, dumbfounded.

'Tell him, Katrine,' Cameron said.

'I emptied the gunpowder out of the bag while you were at the Sheriff's office with Mr. Cameron,' Katrine said in a small voice, 'and then I filled the bag again with a mixture of sulphur, charcoal and salt.'

'It looks exactly like gunpowder,' Cameron took up the tale, 'but, of course, it cannot fire. And that was what you used to reload the pistol that morning.'

'*You* told her to do this!' I accused, glaring at him. 'But how could you know I would reload the pistol!'

Cameron looked at me compassionately. 'It was easy, boy. All I had to do was to create the necessary climate of suspicion by objecting strongly to your having it with you in court, and then to drop that objection after I had taken an obvious opportunity to talk alone with Katrine. You were certain then to suspect that I had told her to tamper with the pistol, and so I knew you would not take the chance of leaving the old charge in it.'

Slowly he put the pistol in his pocket. I felt his eyes on me as I leaned forward and rested my face between my hands, but I could not speak. I was crushed as I had never been in my life before, for the trick that had disarmed me had done more than render the pistol useless. It had shattered my dream – the brave lonely dream that had kept a little spark of defiance alight in me after the flame of it had gone out for the rest of the Greenyards people.

I could see the foolishness of my dream now that I was seeing my fine weapon at last for what it really was – an ancient, outdated pistol so clumsy in its uses that even a girl unused to

155

firearms could tamper undetected with its loading. And because of that I was seeing myself now for what *I* really was – a foolish, deluded boy blindly setting up the tiny barrier of his defiance against forces powerful enough to crush thousands of people without anyone knowing or even caring they had ever existed.

The hot pride that had been in me cooled to an icy sweat of shame in the romantic foolishness of the ideas I had cherished. Yet despite that, I could feel my face still flaming with humiliation between my hands when the carriage came to a halt at last and Mr. Cameron said, 'This is the parting of our ways then, my dears.'

The pity in his eyes when he looked at me was more than I could bear, and if I had not been brought up to think of discourtesy to my elders as unpardonable, I would have left him then without even a shake of the hand. As it was, I made the best thanks I could for all his kindness to us, and took a grave and formal leave of him.

After that I could have made no more effort of any kind. I was beaten, and knew it. I trudged in silence beside Katrine up the Glen Convinth road and through the soft green folds of the hills separating Beauly from Drumnadrochit. The far, lost sound of curlews crying as dusk fell gave voice to the loneliness that was in me, and when we settled down on a bed of heather that night by the shores of Loch Ness the cold, sad voice of the loch water lapping spoke for long to me before I slept, uneasily, at last.

We woke the next morning to a day of shining blue and gold and began the long tramp down the Great Glen to Fort William. Two days and three nights the whole journey took us, and in that time I had added to the shame and bitterness of my defeat the knowledge of the pain it would be to leave my own land for ever.

The weather held the same as on the start of our journey, for September is the month of all the year in the Highlands with mild nights and days of sunshine gilding the bracken and opening the heather-flowers to exploring bees. We walked by day with the blue loch water at our feet and mountains towering around our heads, and it seemed to me then that I had never before seen the bracken shine more brightly gold or the heather spread its purple cloak more royally over the land. And I knew this land was mine, and that I would remember it with longing always.

We slept out in the lee of any shelter we could find, and as we avoided all human habitation by night, so we avoided all meeting with any of the few travellers on the road by day. Neither of us spoke much. We had too much to think about. The rough lying at night began to trouble the old injury in my shoulder so badly that whenever I stumbled over a pothole in the road it wrung a cry from me. Katrine offered to let me lean on her at these times but I refused, thinking shame to let myself be helped by a girl.

We lay the third night just beyond Spean Bridge, and the ache in my shoulder kept me awake for most of that night. I was up at first light urging Katrine on the last few miles to Fort William, and an hour or so after dawn we came into the town.

Neither of us had any idea of where to find the Greenyards people, but we could see that there would be no difficulty about finding the *Good Chance*. The main street of the town ran close to the shore of Loch Linnhe, the big sea loch that made an anchorage for the ocean-going ships. We could see a number of them standing out at anchor in the loch as we walked down the street, and we had not gone far when we came to a side-street that led straight down to the deep-water pier. We hurried down it and stood looking round at the huddle of sheds and warehouses sprawled out along the marshy shore on either side of the pier.

There was a rough sailor-looking fellow leaning against the

door of one of the warehouses. I hailed him and he sauntered towards us. We could hardly understand him at first he had such a curious-sounding English accent, but at least his gestures were clear enough. The *Good Chance* was the ship riding at anchor directly ahead of the pier, and as for the people sailing on her,

'They're 'oled up in there,' he said, pointing to two of the sheds on our left.

We thanked him and went slowly towards the sheds. The door of one was open. As we drew near it we heard a man's voice singing softly in Gaelic.

'That is Ian Mackenzie!' Katrine exclaimed. 'I would know his voice anywhere singing that song!'

She ran to the door calling, 'Ian! Ian Mackenzie! It is Katrine and Connal Ross here!'

I followed more slowly, not quite so sure as she that it was Ian, but before I reached the door he was there hugging Katrine and then holding her at arm's length to look at her and then at myself approaching, and turning his head to shout:

'Look who is here, then! Anne Ross's bairns, no less!'

One head after another poked out through the door, and as Ian came to me with hands outstretched in welcome, men and boys came streaming out of the shed after him. I was surrounded, my hand shaken, my back slapped, my hair ruffled. Someone shouted for the women-folk to be fetched and I saw Angus Ross darting off to another of the sheds.

After that, it was pandemonium for the women and the girls who came running from the other shed were quicker than the men to notice the fine clothes I had acquired and they all tried to ask questions at once. Katrine disappeared, swept away in a swirl of skirts and female chatter. I found myself being swept into the men's shed in the same way and then set down on a hard wooden chair.

'Now,' Ian beamed at me. 'It is a long, long story you have to tell – all six months of it! So let us hear it now, for we are all listening.'

'There is not that much to tell,' I said. 'I just hid out in the Bodach Mhor cave with Katrine all summer, and then we went down to Tain to see the lawyer and he loaned me these clothes so that I could go to the trial without McCaig noticing me.'

'Ah, the trial!' They all glanced at John Ross, Peter Ross's brother.

'I was there too, Connal,' he told me quietly, 'sitting well at the back of the public benches in the downstairs part of the court-room. I got a lift to Inverness and back in a carrier's cart, so I was well ahead of you on the return journey.'

'Peter was good to my mother at the trial,' I said. 'I am sorry the Judge was so hard on him.'

'Aye, he did his best to make up for the charges not being pressed by the Advocate Depute,' John Ross agreed.

'That was a queer business,' Ian Mackenzie said thoughtfully. 'What do you know about it, Connal?'

I told them the story of Cameron's plan. I told them how I had sat there prepared to shoot McCaig if the plan had gone amiss. I told them of McCaig's pursuit and of my useless pistol, shamed though I still was by my own foolishness, for it came to me that I had brought danger to them by my very presence and so they had a right to know the truth of it.

They heard me out to the end without comment, but when I rose and said I was prepared to go rather than be a danger to them, Ian Mackenzie forced me back to my seat with the broad of his hand.

'You will stay right here and board the ship when we do,' he said sternly, 'and if McCaig comes after you we will find a way to deal with him, never fear for that.'

I sank down under his hand and looked round the shed. Straw-covered bunks lined the walls, so close together that a man lying in one would have his face six inches from the boards of the one above it. The floor was crowded with an assortment of personal gear, barrels and sacks of food. The only light in the shed came from a smoky oil lamp and the air of the place smelled damp and foul. I thought of the snug, neat little houses of Greenyards that had been burned to the ground, and wondered if the women in the other shed were living in the same sort of conditions.

'How long have you lived like this? Were there no lodgings to be had in the town?'

I looked inquiringly round their faces, seeing suddenly how gaunt and pale they looked and that some whom I used to know were missing from among them.

'Where are the others?' I asked. 'What has been happening to you all?'

They told me the tale in fits and starts, spreading it out among them. They had not known there would be such a long wait before the ship sailed – that those lodging-house keepers who were not robbers would shun their custom – that there would be so much provisioning needed for the voyage, or that the Fort William merchants would be waiting like corpse-robbers to strip them of their money when they went to buy.

'We have lived like this of necessity,' Ian Mackenzie finished for all of them, 'finding what labouring work we could to keep from starving before the ship sailed. As for the missing ones, a few had kin-folk they could go to, and some – the older ones especially – could not survive in the bitter weather it was at the time of the clearance.'

'Others died too, for no reason that we could see,' John Ross put in quietly, 'but I think it may have been because their hearts were broken.'

To anyone else this would have sounded fanciful, but I was one of their own kind, I could remember my grandfather crying out by the light of the torches his warning that some of us would sicken and die of grief if we were forced from the glen.

160

I remembered the long pain of my own leave-taking as Katrine and I walked down the Great Glen, and John Ross's words did not seem fanciful to me.

Some of the boys from my own township had edged in to stand close and stare at me while all the talking and explaining was going on. The Munro twins, Donald and Ewan were there, along with Murdo Ross and his cousin, Angus, and I realized how oddly different I must be seeming to them from the Connal they had known in Greenyards. I smiled at the twins. They grinned awkwardly back at me, and I said over their heads to Angus:

'Remember disputing with Mr. Aird over me on the Bodach Mhor, Angus?' He nodded, not smiling as the others were, and I asked, 'Where is he now, then?'

'He stayed on at Ardgay,' Angus said. 'We asked him to come with us but his courage stops short at putting pen to paper. It will not stand the dangers of a sea voyage or the rigours of a new land!'

'Now then, Angus,' one of the men said warningly, 'Mr. Aird is a good man but he is a scholar and you cannot expect such to share the hardships we must face.'

Angus curled his lip scornfully and I could see that it was only the habit of courtesy in him that held him back from arguing the point. Our eyes met, and I thought I saw in his the same bitterness that was in myself.

The twins bent close to me and Ewan whispered, 'Naomi Ross – you remember Naomi Ross from our township, Connal – well, her wits have gone from her since she was beaten over the head by McCaig and then half-drowned in the Carron.'

'She sits and stares at nothing all day,' Donald added, 'and she has to be led everywhere by the hand like a bairn.'

I drew back in horror from them. Naomi – the witless one – she had been the lively, fleet-footed girl running pace by pace with me through the clear dawn of the morning the Sheriff had come upon us! These pale, starved-looking creatures whispering of her fate had been the brown-faced, hardy boys who had marched with me behind Rory Ruadh to take up our first watch on the hill. And these gaunt men – these landless, dispossessed ones crowded into this evil-smelling shed, they had been farmers and soldiers, heritors of a proud blood-line that had lasted for five hundred years. They had been the Rosses of Greenyards. And now?

Now, I thought, there must be laughter in hell over what had become of us all!

I glanced again at Angus Ross. He looked older than his seventeen years, and his face had a hard, bitter look that I could not remember seeing on it before. Then I recalled that we always used to tease him about being sweet on Naomi Ross, and I realized there was one at least among the Greenyards people whose hatred of McCaig could match my own.

And the others, I thought, they all had their own scores to settle with McCaig. He would not take me easily now.

14 *It is not within your warrant to shoot any of my passengers*

Katrine and I wasted no time that day in booking our passage aboard the *Good Chance,* but I took the precaution of signing myself as 'Connal MacIan' on the shipping agent's register. It was no lie to sign myself thus 'Mac' or 'son of' Ian, for my father's Christian name is Ian, and I considered that the change of name would further help to conceal the fact of my sailing on the *Good Chance.*

Katrine was inclined to think all this caution unnecessary now but I could remember only too clearly Mr. Cameron saying of McCaig, 'He has a nose like a bloodhound for a fugitive', and I knew that I was acting wisely.

The rest of that day was spent in shopping for the provisions we would need to last us for the seven weeks of the voyage. They cost us dear, as the Greenyards people had warned us they would do, and we were down to our last shilling before Katrine had got everything on her list. After that the stores had to be carried down to the pier to be ferried out to the *Good Chance* along with those of the other Greenyards people. It was wearisome work loading the boats, and I was glad when that day was finished and the women called us to their quarters for our evening meal.

Their shed was no different from the one occupied by the men except that it was cleaner and neater and they had made some brave attempts to disguise the worst of its squalor. I looked around it as the women served the food and my eye came to rest on Naomi Ross sitting on an upturned box in one corner of the shed.

I had not seen her since the moment McCaig had struck her under the waters of the Carron and I stared at her, curiously at first, and then with pity. She had been a very lively girl, Naomi, with big blue eyes and a pretty habit of tossing her head to throw her hair back over her shoulder.

She was not lively now. She sat still and straight on her box, staring straight in front of her with her wide blue eyes as empty of life as those of a blind girl. Her hands were folded quietly in her lap, and for all the notice she took of it the bustle going on around her might never have existed.

Angus Ross came and sat down beside me. I turned towards him but he was looking at Naomi and before I could speak he said, 'If I get the chance I will kill the man who did that to her.'

Quietly he spoke, so that anyone watching him might have thought he was only passing the time of day, but I knew then that I had guessed correctly about him and Dugald McCaig. That was one Sheriff-Officer who would not survive for two minutes if he met with Angus Ross on a dark night!

I went back to the men's shed that night feeling very low in spirits over Naomi and with a blinding headache added to the rest of my aches. The headache persisted during the next two days that I worked with the men at loading the stores, and on our fourth day in Fort William – our last before we sailed on the morning of the 21st, I woke to find tender swellings under my jaw, my throat so dry that I could barely swallow, and my skin hot with fever.

164

I swung my legs over the side of the bunk, and pain struck me like a clenched fist on the top of my skull. The walls of the shed reeled inwards on me, and the next thing I knew I was being laid back in my bunk and told to stay there till we were ready to sail.

I had no choice but to do as I was told, and all day I lay there with the fever mounting in me. The traffic of the shed went on about me. Katrine looked in briefly to see me. I dozed and woke and dozed again, with all the people who had been concerned with me in the past six months wandering like shadows through my mind. Blind John, my mother, Rory Ruadh, Lachlan Chisholm, Mr. Aird, Mr. Cameron – all the people I had relied on for courage and help floated mistily through my mind and disappeared again as they had disappeared, one by one, out of my life.

Only McCaig was left, a gross black figure shadowing my fevered dreams as he had shadowed my waking hours since I drew the pistol on him in Greenyards. No one had seen or heard anything of him since Katrine and I arrived in Fort William, yet still he invaded my mind as I dozed, and I struggled with him, fighting fiercely against the noose he was trying to force round my neck. But McCaig was determined to have his revenge and he was too strong for me —!

I called hoarsely for help, shouting out to the men of Greenyards to stand by me against the Law, and the men of Greenyards answered me. A light shone in my eyes. I heard the sound of feet tramping and the rumble of voices, and blinking against the light I wakened to the sight of Angus Ross and Ian Mackenzie bending over me. John Ross hovered behind them. It was night. The lamp was lit, and the shed was empty except for myself and these three.

'We have bad news, Connal,' Ian said. 'Can you understand us, or has the fever too strong a grip on you?'

Hoarsely I asked, 'Is it McCaig?'

'He is on board the *Good Chance* now,' Angus said, 'and he will be staying on her till every man, woman and child is embarked tomorrow.'

'Standing at the head of the ladder we will all have to climb to get aboard,' Ian took up the tale, 'and searching every face that passes him.'

I was too confused to grasp it properly at first. 'Why wait on the ship? Why does he not come here to arrest me? He must know the rest of you are here!'

'He probably does,' Ian said. 'In which case he will know also that he could not take you without us putting up a strong resistance.'

'The ship is the surest way for him,' Angus added. 'He can have you at pistol-point as you come up the ladder, and the Captain of the ship there to back up his authority.'

'You are only confusing the boy,' John Ross put in. He shouldered his way between the other two. 'Tell him how we know about McCaig, Ian, and just how much we *do* know.'

'It was an hour ago we were having a bit of a talk with the Captain about the voyage,' Ian said. 'He told us there was a Sheriff-Officer came aboard this afternoon with two constables and a warrant to search the ship for a boy called Connal Ross that pulled a pistol on him and tried to kill him. Well, of course, you were not there, and so McCaig – it must be McCaig, it could be no other – said he would stay aboard till the last passenger was embarked. The Captain was not well pleased to have a Sheriff-Officer parading his authority aboard his ship but there was nothing he could do about it in the face of McCaig's warrant.

'We dared not show our interest by asking too many questions,' John Ross added, 'and so we have no idea how much McCaig knows of your whereabouts. You booked your passage as "Connal MacIan" after all and so he cannot be certain that you mean to sail on the *Good Chance*. In fact, the likelihood is that when he failed to find you in Tain he only came through to Fort William on the strength of a guess that you would be with us.'

'It makes no difference,' I said wearily. 'I am too sick to run away and if I go aboard I will walk straight into his arms.' I turned away from them. 'Leave me be and get ready to sail yourselves.'

Angus grasped my arm and pulled me round to face them again. 'Wait! We have worked out a plan to get you aboard. All we need is a rope, a set of bagpipes, a boat and someone to row it. John Ross here has the pipes, and Ian knows where we can get a boat and an oarsman. Now, listen!'

I listened and he explained the plan. When he had finished, Ian said, 'The main thing to remember is this. The ship is due to sail at high tide which is at four o'clock tomorrow morning. If the Captain misses that tide there will not be enough current to carry him through the Corran Narrows and out into the open Atlantic. He will be caught in the narrows and the ship will be at the mercy of the dangerous currents there, and so he dare not risk delaying the sailing. That is why the timing of the plan is so important.'

'Does Katrine know of this?' I asked.

'None of the women know and we are not going to let them know – least of all Katrine,' Ian said. 'What she does not know she cannot tell – however she may be questioned about you.'

As if she had been summoned by the mention of her own name Katrine appeared at the door of the shed at that moment. She had a bowl in her hand and she came towards me with it.

'You are to try and sup this now, Connal,' she said. 'And you three, will you go for your supper with the rest of the men? We want the dishes cleared up.'

I waved the bowl away. 'No, no, I cannot swallow.'

'Ah, try a little,' she coaxed. 'You will not be strong enough to get aboard if you do not eat.'

Ian took the bowl from her and thrust it at me. 'Come now, eat up when you are told!' He frowned warningly at me. I took the bowl and made to sup from it. 'There you are!' He turned smiling to Katrine. 'You see, there is no need to worry about him. You go with the rest of the women. They will have their hands full with the bairns and you can look after Naomi for them. We will see Connal safely aboard.'

Katrine hesitated, looking worriedly at me. I raised a smile for her and she made up her mind. 'Yes, of course. He will be fine with you.' She moved to the door. 'Well, are you three coming for your supper?'

'Yes. Yes, indeed,' Ian said hastily. He threw me a meaning look. 'We will be back shortly, Connal.'

I watched them out and then put down the bowl. I tried to think but my mind refused to work. All I could see was Mc-Caig standing at the head of the boarding-ladder, a pistol in his hand. If only I had not given up my own pistol —! But what good could it have done me now, anyway? To shoot McCaig under these circumstances would only mean jeopardizing the passage of the rest of the Greenyards people to the Americas. Ian's plan was by far the better course.

The rest of the men and boys began to come back into the shed. From the few words they exchanged with me I gathered that they knew the position and were prepared for the part they had to play. The other three must have passed the word quietly to them on their way back from the women's shed.

I do not know if any of the others in the shed with me slept during the few hours that were left to us. Ian, John Ross and Angus went straight to their bunks when they came back from the women's shed. The lamp had already been turned down low and I could see nothing but the black shapes of the figures in the bunks. They might have been as wide awake as myself for all I knew, and I think that they were for they lay too still for natural sleep.

Ian was the first to rise again. He came over to the lamp, turned up the wick and said loudly:

'Three o'clock and time to rise!'

The dark shapes swung feet to the floor. Ewan Munro was sent running to tell the women to assemble on the pier. Angus caught my arm as I came blundering out of my bunk, and helped me on with my shoes and jacket. Ian was winding a length of half-inch rope round his waist. He threw his plaid over his shoulder and drew the ends of it round his waist to conceal the rope.

'Ready?' he asked.

Angus nodded. 'Aye. Take his other arm and we'll manage him between us.'

He took a firm hold of my left arm. Ian grasped my right arm and they steered me out of the door. It was still dark outside and the groups of Greenyards people hurrying to the pier carried lanterns to guide them along it. Ian and Angus bore to the right, away from the pier. The ground underfoot was marshy. I suppose it must have sucked at our feet but I could not truthfully say I had any sensation of walking at all. I seemed to float, with my head miles away from my feet and having no connection with the rest of me.

I heard Ian mutter, 'He is far gone in the fever,' and Angus reply, 'We will manage it so long as he does not fall unconscious altogether,' but it was only vaguely that I realized they were talking about myself.

Our feet rang out suddenly loud. I looked down and realized we were walking along a spit of rock. The water of the loch lapped on either side of it. There was a boat at the end of the spit. There were two figures in it, a man and a boy. The man stood up as we reached the boat, and helped Ian and Angus to pass me into it. I plumped down on one of the thwarts beside the boy. He was only half my size and I wondered stupidly what he was doing there. Then I remembered the rope.

Ian was talking to the boatman. 'Remember the signal, now,' he was saying, *'Cha till mi tuille* – We shall return no more!'

The boatman grunted. 'Cast off,' he told the boy. Ian and Angus gave the boat a push as the boy drew in the rope that had held it to a post driven into a crevice of the rock. The boatman pulled and we shot out over the loch.

The boat bore to the right in a wide circle away from the *Good Chance*. Lights moved on the pier to our left, and as we swung into the arc that was to bring us up eventually against the far side of the ship, I saw the first of the boats loaded with the Greenyards people shoot out from the pier and begin the pull to the ship's near side.

She looked enormous to me but I had no knowledge of ocean-going ships by which to judge. Her deck was well-lit and I could clearly make out figures moving about it, sailors working in the rigging, and a small knot of men standing at the head of the boarding-ladder.

'They will see us with all that light about,' I muttered.

'No danger,' the boatman said. 'You can see them because you are looking into the light. They cannot see us so long as we keep out of its range.'

The boy asked, 'Why are you on the run, mister?'

'Hold your wheesht, you,' the boatman growled. 'It's no fault of his he's on the run and that is all *you* need to know.'

He shipped his oars and let the current running up the loch carry us out to the widest point of our arc. I kept my eyes on the boats moving out to the ship while we drifted like this. There were people mounting the boarding-ladder from the first boat to close with the ship's side, and each one who arrived on deck had to pass through the little knot of men standing at the top of the ladder.

The boatman was watching also. As the first boat turned

empty away from the ship and the second one moved in to take its place, he bent to his oars again and started on the second half of the arc that would finish up on the ship's far side. He was rowing across the current now and he had to pull hard. I began to dread that our timing would go amiss and that we would arrive too late for the signal.

The second boat disappeared from my view as we began to swing inwards to close with the ship. This was the boat Ian and Angus would be on, and there were two more to disembark passengers after it was empty. We were still on time – providing nothing went wrong!

The boatman rowed with long, steady strokes, the leaping slap of the tide-water covering the swishing sound of his oars. The dark bulk of the ship's side drew nearer and nearer. He glanced back and shortened his stroke before closing with it. The boy leaned out over the gunwale, a padded stanchion in his hand. As the ship's side loomed over us, the boy fended us off with his stanchion and the boatman finned his oars to hold us steady. The boy rose to his feet, swaying and groping along the ship's side.

'I have it!' His voice came floating down to us in a whisper. Cautiously then he lowered himself back down beside me, the rope he had gripped clenched in his right hand. The slack of it fell into his lap. Deftly he slid it through his fingers, looped it round me and knotted it at my waist.

'Take a grip of it beyond the slack,' he whispered.

I fumbled along the slack and clenched my hands round the part of the rope falling straight from the ship's side. Now it was myself who was anchoring the boat with the rope round my body. Boy and boatman expertly changed places, and the boy kept an oar finning while the boatman steadied us still further by laying hold of the rope along with me.

A strange confusion of sounds came down to us and mingled in our ears with the slap of the water against the ship's side.

Voices, and feet tramping, sounds of swishing, rattling, and flapping, and over it all an occasional shouted order in seaman's language. Some officer giving commands to the sailors, I thought, and glancing at the boatman saw that he was listening intently to the various commands. He felt my eyes on him and nodded towards the ship.

'They are ready for the tide to swing about,' he whispered. 'That means your people should be bringing their last boat alongside any second now.'

Hard on his words, the signal came. The brief tuning up of the pipes first, and then the surge of the melody as John Ross launched into *Cha till mi tuille*. Loud and shrill and so piercingly melancholy that the hair rose on my neck, the pipes called out across the loch. A tremor ran down the rope.

'Grip hard!' the boatman whispered. Half-rising he put his hands round my waist and steadied me as I rose with the tightening pull on the rope from above. My feet scraped over the gunwale of the boat. It bobbed away from under me and I was left hanging free against the ship's side.

I held on to the rope with the grip of a drowning man and was raised slowly in a long, steady pull till my head and shoulders rose above the bulwark. Hands clutched my shoulders, and heaved. I came up waist-high to the bulwark and hung across it for a second before the hands toppled me over. As I landed on the deck behind a screen of men's bodies, a girl screamed, harsh and shrill. There was a violent flurry of movement among the men pressing around and in front of me and a voice from among them said desperately:

'*Hold on to Angus!*'

The mass of bodies heaved with internal struggle. The girl was still screaming. As I scrambled to my feet a body thudded back beside me against the bulwark – Angus Ross, pinned by one man, silenced with a hand held over his mouth by another. The screen of bodies shifted and broke with the movement. I peered through the gap. Ian Mackenzie's arm swung heavily across my chest forcing me back out of sight, but I still had an oblique view of the scene on the deck in front of me.

It was Naomi Ross screaming. She stood as if clamped to the deck, her face turned towards McCaig standing at the top of the boarding-ladder. Her hands clutched her head and her mouth was frozen open in scream after scream of horror. The deck was crowded with passengers but they had all shrunk back from the madness the sight of McCaig seemed to have brought upon her.

McCaig was looking at her, grinning, but in the second that I peered out from behind Ian he turned back to look towards a girl stepping from the ladder on to the deck. The constable beside him raised his lantern. The girl turned her face into the light. I glimpsed Katrine blinking, white and startled, at the scene on deck as McCaig roared, 'There is the girl who was with him at the trial!' and then everything seemed to happen at once.

McCaig grabbed Katrine with his left hand, his right hand with a pistol in it flashed up to her head. Naomi launched herself bodily forward, her fingers clawing for McCaig's eyes. Angus burst free, roaring, from the hold that was on him and leapt after the two constables closing in on McCaig and the girls.

A shot rang out. The struggling bodies broke apart. Angus staggered out from the group with his arm round Naomi's shoulders. Katrine reappeared, sagging slowly to her knees in front of McCaig. His gun hung loosely in his hand. A curl of smoke rose up from the barrel as he stared down at Katrine.

A roar of sound came from the crowd on deck as the group broke apart. Ian Mackenzie's arm was still across my chest, blocking the move I tried to make to Katrine. I pushed against it, shouting to him to stand clear, but before the words were well out of my mouth he had his hand over my face and was bearing me back against the bulwark as the other man had done with Angus. The Greenyards men moved in to cover the vacant space Ian's move left in their ranks.

The voice of command I had heard earlier shouted, 'Make way there, and let me see what has happened!'

'The Captain!' Ian hissed in my ear. 'If I let you go will you keep quiet while he deals with McCaig?'

My answer was to fight madly against the heavy bulk of him prisoning me to the bulwark, but the fever defeated me and my resistance was brief. Ian felt the strength go out of me.

'She is not badly hurt,' he whispered. 'I saw from the way she fell. Will you keep quiet now?'

I had not the strength left to do anything else. I nodded. He took his hand away from my mouth and stepped back. I sagged against the bulwark and he held me up, with his arm supporting my shoulders. The noise on deck had died down and now the Captain's voice could clearly be heard calling:

'Tell Dr. Hamilton to come here quickly. This young woman needs a surgeon!'

Ian shuffled forward a step or two with me so that we could peer out past the heads and shoulders of the men in front of us. I saw the Captain straightening up from Katrine's huddled figure lying on the deck. He turned to McCaig and said angrily:

'You have something here to answer for, Mister! It is not within your warrant to shoot any of my passengers.'

'The pistol was discharged by accident in the struggle when the mad-woman sprang at me,' McCaig retorted. 'And in any case, the girl is an accomplice of the boy named in my warrant. If she is here it means that he must be somewhere aboard also, and I intend to search the ship until I find him.'

The Captain was a small man, especially seen beside Mc-Caig's bulky stature. There was no doubting his authority, however, as he drew himself up and said icily:

'Mister, I am under orders to sail with the outgoing tide.

The tide is with me now and I have an off-shore breeze. I have already complied with your warrant for search and I do not intend to endanger my ship by missing the tide while you repeat that search. You will please to take yourself and your men ashore.'

'I will leave this ship only when I have made certain that Connal Ross is not aboard,' McCaig repeated stubbornly.

The Captain shrugged. 'Very well. Stay aboard if you please.'

McCaig holstered his pistol and beckoned to the two constables. As they started across the deck towards him the Captain cupped his hands to his mouth and shouted:

'Weigh anchor!'

'W-e-igh anchor!'

The repetition of the command went echoing down the ship. The constables halted in their stride and looked questioningly from McCaig to the Captain.

'I delay my sailing for no one,' he told McCaig curtly. 'Let us hope you have a pleasant trip to the Americas while you search, Mister!'

He turned on his heel, leaving McCaig glaring in speechless fury after him. The crowd on deck surged in a dozen different directions out of the path of the sailors leaping to fill the commands that followed thick and fast on the Captain's first order. I lost sight of McCaig but Ian could still see over the heads of those in front of us. As the ship shuddered and heaved into life he exclaimed, 'The Captain has beaten him, Connal. He is going over the side!'

He whirled me round to face himself, gripping me hard and exultantly by the shoulders. 'You are free now, Connal! You have seen the last of McCaig!'

I could feel none of the exultation that was in him. Katrine had been shot. She was still lying there on the deck and I had to get to her. I brushed feebly at Ian's hands. He let me go and I staggered forward, swaying and pushing my way towards the spot where she lay.

I found her half-sitting, half-lying across the lap of one of our own women. One sleeve of her dress, slit from wrist to shoulder and soaked with blood, hung down on the deck beside her. The Captain was bending over her, and on his knees beside her a young man was rolling a bandage neatly round her upper arm.

I dropped to my knees also, beside her. But not from choice, for I do not think I could have stood upright for a second longer. The young man was talking, in the accents of the Lowlands, to the Captain, and through the fog of fever in my brain I heard him say:

'...and not two minutes on the ship before they are the cause of violence! But what can you expect of wild creatures like these Highlanders? They are still mostly savages at heart for all the attempts that have been made to tame them. Just savages!'

They say that the whole of a drowning man's life passes in front of his eyes in the second before he dies, but I do not know the truth of that. All I know is that in the second I struggled to lift my head to protest against the surgeon's words, the whole story of our brave and useless resistance in Greenyards passed before my mind's sight. My head came up and I looked full into the surgeon's face.

His eyes swept me in a long, cold stare of contempt for the picture I presented, and hatred rose in me against this Lowlander so calmly passing his judgment on us. I hated him for his ignorance of us, his arrogance, his calm dismissal of all we had suffered. I tried to tell him so, but there was a darkness creeping over my brain and my tongue refused to obey me.

I felt myself sinking to the deck beside Katrine, but even though I knew then that I might die without the Lowland doctor's aid, my last thought before I fainted completely away was that I hated the very look of him.

15 Do not expect me to play traitor

'I hated the very look of him ...'

I stared down at the words I had just written, wondering where it was I had seen them before or heard them spoken. The ring of them was so familiar to me and yet it was a moment or two before I remembered that this last, fainting thought of mine had also been the first one to cross my mind when I saw Dr. Hamilton walking towards me on my first day on deck after the fever left me.

I pushed the paper away from me and sat trying to recapture the interval in between – the time I had lain in the dimness below decks in a confusion of strange noises and fevered dreams. Dr. Hamilton had appeared in my dreams – or at least, I had thought so at the time. I remembered hazily seeing him bending over me. I remembered the soft, burring sound of his Lowland voice and the touch of hard, cold fingers that came with it.

Later on, when the fever had left me and before I was strong enough to rise from my bunk, I had watched him moving about in the half-light in our quarters tending other figures crying out in the delirium of fever, and Katrine had whispered to me that it was the typhus he was fighting. The filthy sheds we had been herded into at Fort William had been the cause of it, and myself the first to go down before it.

I had been too weak to think or feel anything at all during that time of partial recovery, and it was only on my first day on deck that the sight of Dr. Hamilton had brought the past all rushing back to me. I had remembered instantly the arrogant Lowland judgment he had passed on us, and the hatred born in that moment had taken sudden command of my mind again.

My eyes wandered back to the paper in front of me – Hamilton's paper. I let Hamilton's pen drop from my hand and stared round the cabin where I had sat scribbling every day for four weeks.

It seemed incredible to me at that moment when I came full circle in my story but it was true, nevertheless, that I knew Hamilton scarcely any better than I had when he first sat me down at his desk and told me to write. He had come and gone again so quietly at all the times he had been in the cabin with me, and I had been too absorbed in my story to do more than reply very briefly to any greeting he gave me.

There had been no attempt to force conversation on me, no attempt to pry into what I had written. Dr. Hamilton had left me so severely alone that his servant might have been excused for thinking that the cabin belonged to me and not to the doctor. But now all that was finished, for I had come to the end of my story and all that remained for me to do was to parcel up my papers for him to read when we reached the Americas. That was my part of the bargain – the payment I had agreed on for the use of his cabin and the materials with which to write my story.

How would it appear to him? I wondered. For that matter, how would it appear to myself?

I had not re-read one word of the many I had written since

the day I took the pen from Dr. Hamilton's hand, for I had so clear a memory of all the events which had taken place that there had been no need for me to stop and think what I should write. Indeed, the words had poured so fast and fluently from me that my mind had outrun my pen many times, and for all I knew the manuscript in front of me might read like nonsense to anyone who did not know Greenyards.

I turned back the pages rapidly, stopping to read a bit here and a bit there, but I soon saw that this would be no way to judge the whole and settled down to read the story from beginning to end. It took me two hours to do so, and long before I reached the last page I was painfully aware of how far I had departed from my original purpose.

I had set out to show the injustice that had been done to the Greenyards people and to tell of their courage in the face of it, and in fairness to myself I had to admit that I had succeeded in this to some extent in the part of the story that dealt with our resistance to the serving of the writs of eviction. Even this, however, was so highly coloured with my own thoughts and feelings that there was little room in it for anyone else. As for the rest of the story —!

I looked up from the paper with my cheeks burning with shame. The rest of the story was nothing more than a recital of my own adventures, a long cry of protest against my own wrongs. I had let everything else but the telling of them slip from my mind, and I sat back appalled at the conceit which had led me to think that I was the one who should write the Greenyards story.

The last dregs of my ambition to succeed where the journalist Donald Ross had failed, drained away with the bursting bubble of my conceit. For how could this jumble of boy's emotions, this breathless account of my running battle with McCaig be taken for the protest against injustice and the cry for truth I had intended my story to be?

I got up from the desk and stood there with my knuckles pressed against it, my head hanging down. I had failed – failed so utterly that all I wanted to do now was to get quickly away from the evidence of my failure. I moved slowly round the desk towards the cabin door. It opened before I could reach it and Dr. Hamilton appeared. I stood aside to let him pass. He nodded his usual greeting to me, his eyes travelling past me to the desk.

'Your papers,' he reminded me. 'You are forgetting them.'

I had never left them on the desk before but always taken them back to our own quarters with me, jealously guarding them there from even Katrine's eyes. I took a step now to the desk at his reminder, but my lifted hand dropped again to my side before it touched the papers.

'I have finished,' I told him. 'There is no more to write.'

'Ah, but our bargain was that I should not read it before we reached the Americas!' he said cheerfully. 'You were afraid I would play Judas on the hero of Greenyards – remember?'

The jeer in the word 'hero' was so much an echo of my own scorn of the way I had portrayed myself in the story that it might have been chosen on purpose to complete my humiliation. I had no defence left now against anything he might say, and I did not even care any longer what he did with the information the story gave him about myself. I faced up to him, groping for the shreds of my pride so that I could speak with dignity.

'Read the papers any time you like,' I told him. 'They may serve whatever purpose you had in mind when you gave me the freedom of your desk, but they will not serve mine and so there is no point in my holding them from you till we reach the Americas.'

I turned away from him but he moved quickly between me and the door and asked, 'When do you wish them returned to you?'

'Never!'

'Never?'

I met his puzzled look squarely. 'You spoke the world's opinion of us when you called us savages,' I said bitterly. 'You spoke Sheriff Taylor's opinion, and that of the Judge who tried my mother. You spoke for all the respectable Lowlanders and Englishmen who hate and fear the Highlander because he is different from them. You spoke for all the clever men who cannot understand why we should want to cling to our ancient way of life when there is money to be made from a new one – for those who do not know that we despise money and prize loyalty above all things —'

'Wait a moment, Connal —' he began, but I swept on over his words:

'You spoke for all those who do not know and would not care if they did know that our language is as old as the mountains we once lived in, or that the songs and poems we have made from it are as many and as sweet as the sound of our rivers. You spoke for all those who do not know and do not care that our race is being destroyed, our people scattered and our language lost so that a few men can become rich off the backs of sheep.

'Sheep!' I repeated scornfully, and glared at him, daring him to speak. He said nothing, but somehow the look on his face was very like the one Mr. Cameron had given me when we parted at Beauly. All my anger left me, and the shame I had felt earlier returned in full force.

'I thought I could write the true story of Greenyards,' I said quietly, 'so that any who read it would hear in it the voice of truth and a great cry for justice for my people.'

'But you *have* told the story.' Hamilton looked towards the desk. 'You say it is finished.'

'Yes, it is finished and I háve failed in what I set out to do. I was so taken up with my own part in the story that I lost sight of the main purpose and wrote mostly of myself. And people are not interested in a boy's adventures, Dr. Hamilton. There is no argument for truth and justice in such trivial things. So let me go now and do what you wish with the papers. I do not care any longer what happens when we reach the Americas.'

Dr. Hamilton stepped aside. I went through the door without another look at him and climbed slowly to the upper deck. Katrine was there, leaning over the bulwark with her hair streaming out behind her in the breeze of the ship's passage, but I did not want to speak to her then and I turned quickly away to avoid her.

She must have been watching for me, however, for as I went rapidly along the deck she came after me, calling my name. I waited reluctantly till she came up with me.

'Have you seen him – Dr. Hamilton?' she asked breathlessly. 'Has he spoken to you?'

I stared, puzzled by her excited manner. 'He spoke to me about my writing, yes. But what —'

'Oh, Connal, you are impossible!' Tears of vexation sprang up in Katrine's eyes and she swung away from me to stand with her arms folded and one foot tapping on the deck. I waited for her to speak again, still puzzled to know what it was all about, but thinking it best to keep quiet in view of the signs of her anger.

She swung round on me again after a few moments of this. 'This writing has got between you and your wits,' she said sharply, 'or else you would know what everyone else on the ship knows by now – that Dr. Hamilton has been courting me these three weeks past!'

'Oh, is that it!' I smiled at her, relieved, and amused to think of the disappointment that waited the Lowlander. 'Well then, you will have the pleasure of refusing him when he asks for your hand!'

'I have had the honour of accepting his proposal,' she told

182

me icily, 'as you would know by now if you had let him speak as he wanted when he came down to see you in his cabin a few minutes ago.'

Angrily I seized her by the shoulders. 'I'll not permit it, do you hear! I'll not let my sister play traitor to her own blood-kin!'

'Let go, Connal, you are hurting me.' Katrine spoke very quietly and I dropped my hands, ashamed of my violence but still boiling with anger against her and Hamilton.

'You cannot marry him,' I said sullenly. 'He is different from us, different as night from day. He cannot even speak our language, Katrine.'

'I can speak *his* language,' she pointed out. 'And in any case, we are both Scottish for all he is Lowland and I am High-land. That will create a bond stronger than the difference between us once we are both exiles in a strange land.'

I had not known that Hamilton intended to settle in the Americas also, but I let that pass and reminded her, 'You said you would marry a Highlander like yourself – if you married at all!'

Katrine laughed. 'I have grown up a little since then! I have discovered that you do not choose whom you are to love.'

I walked away from her and stood leaning over the bulwark gazing down at the water slipping past the ship's side. Katrine came and stood beside me and put her hand on my shoulder.

'You will forget when you have married him,' I said, not looking at her. 'You have half-forgotten it all already.'

'You are too bitter, Connal,' she told me gently. 'It is better to forget.'

'*I* will not forget!' I whirled round on her. 'Go, marry your Lowlander! Line yourself up alongside the Sheriffs and the Judges and the rich sheep-men! Go, forget your blood-ties and your language and your land, but do not expect me to play traitor along with you!'

Poor Katrine! She could not have been more shocked if I had struck her in the face, but my bitterness at her treachery to our cause was too great to let me feel regret at my words. I stalked away from her, unheeding the plaintive cry she sent after me, and went down to the emigrant quarters.

They were, as usual, crowded with all the discomfort of more than four hundred people trying to live in a space designed for three hundred, and the Greenyards people were no better off in this respect than the other emigrants. I picked my way through baskets and cooking-pots and playing children to where Ian Mackenzie was hammering away at the slats of a broken bunk, and shouted to him through the din:

'How long now till we sight land, Ian?'

Ian swung round in astonishment at the sound of my voice, for it was the first time since I had started writing that I had put in an appearance in our quarters through the day.

'Three days, I think, according to the calendar Angus is keeping,' he said, eyeing me curiously before he turned and shouted:

'Angus! How many days now till·we sight land?'

'Angus!' a girl's voice repeated his call. 'Where are you? Someone is wanting our landing date!'

I turned to Ian in astonishment. 'That's Naomi Ross's voice!'

'If you had not been living with your head in the clouds you would not be so surprised to hear it!' Ian said tartly.

'But is she not still —'

'No, she is not. Something happened to her that morning she came so suddenly face to face with McCaig again. She has been her normal self since then, and according to Dr. Hamilton it was the shock of seeing him so unexpectedly that brought her back into her wits, the same way she was shocked out of them by his attack on her. He has seen such things happen

184

before, he says, but it is a great wonder and cause for thankful-ness, all the same.'

'Three days' sailing we have yet to do – is that what you were asking?' Angus's voice came from behind me.

I turned to look at the calendar in his hand and saw Naomi standing beside him. She smiled at me and tossed her hair back in the gesture I remembered.

'Were you talking about Dr. Hamilton? He is a good doctor, and kind too.'

'He is that,' Angus agreed. 'There's a few of the typhus cases would never have seen the Americas if he had not worked day and night on them.'

And I was one of them, I thought, as I went on deck again. Katrine had said I would have been at the bottom of the Atlantic now if it had not been for his doctoring.

I had never thanked him for that, and no doubt he thought me mannerless and ungrateful. As indeed I was, but it is very difficult to accept favours from the hand of an enemy, and so long as I thought of Hamilton in this way I could not bring myself to give him the thanks that were his due.

I avoided him altogether, in fact, for the short time that remained of the voyage. I took good care to be out of the emigrant quarters when he was paying his daily visit there, and whenever we happened to be on deck at the same time I kept as much of the ship as possible between us. I had plenty of time for this sort of thing – too much time, in fact, for I no longer had my writing to occupy me and no Katrine to help me while away the empty hours of sailing over empty seas.

She was always in Hamilton's company now, walking the deck with him, leaning over the ship's side to watch the sea while they laughed at some private joke, or sitting talking quietly together in a sheltered corner by one of the boats.

I saw the flutter of my manuscript in his hands once or twice while they sat like this, and guessing that they must be discussing it, I thought to myself that at least Katrine would be able to assure Hamilton that I had written the truth.

The thought brought some measure of satisfaction to me. I had tried and failed to write the Greenyards story in the form it deserved, and so now no one would ever know of the boys and girls who had stood watch on Ardgay Hill, the men who had toiled over the work of a fighting withdrawal, the women who had gathered to parley and play for time. The great cry for justice that I had meant to try and form from it all had somehow petered out into the details of my own small part in the story, but I *had* told the truth as I saw it. And in that, at least, I had been faithful to the spirit of Greenyards.

I was on deck at the moment the American mainland was sighted. The same feeling of expectancy that had drawn many of the other emigrants to the upper deck had taken me there also, but strain as I might I could not see the line of land which everyone else hoped to see that day.

'You will hear the sailor at the mast-head call out the sight of land before you can see it from here,' Hamilton's voice said behind me, and then Katrine's voice came:

'I wonder, will it look so very different from Scotland?'

Hamilton laughed and said something I could not catch. I stood there resenting their presence, but unwilling to be so rude as to walk away while Katrine was there.

There was a tap on my shoulder and then Hamilton said, 'You have not yet congratulated me on winning Katrine's hand!'

I turned round. 'I do not intend to,' I told him. 'I do not approve my sister marrying a Lowlander.'

'No one who reads your story could expect otherwise,' he acknowledged wryly.

'You will know now, then, why I classed Lowlanders

187

like yourself along with the English oppressors of the Highlands.'

'Aye, your story was a revelation to me. It will be a revelation to many people when they read it.'

'No one will ever read the story of Greenyards now – I told you that,' I said flatly.

Hamilton laughed, but sobered again immediately he saw the look on my face.

'Forgive me, Connal,' he said, 'but you have all the over-earnestness of the very young, and I am afraid you have all their misconceptions about their elders, too. I am sorry that —'

'And I am glad I do not share your views,' I interrupted stiffly. 'There is nothing at all amusing to me in the death of a way of life or the destruction of a people.'

The expression on Hamilton's face changed abruptly to one of exasperation.

'Will you be quiet!' he roared. 'I am trying to apologize to you!' He glared indignantly at me. 'I am not blind or deaf, you know! I have had plenty of opportunity to see how wrong I was in my opinions of you Highland people. I admit it, and I apologize. So now will you be quiet and listen to what else I have to say!'

Astonishment so robbed me of speech at this that I could only nod, but Hamilton took this as sufficient reply and in a more reasonable tone he added, 'Of course you cannot be blamed for thinking as you do, for heaven knows you have good cause to be bitter. But what you do not see, Connal, what you may not be able to see perhaps till you are older – although it comes plainly through your story and has been made clear to me also through what I have observed in the past seven weeks – is that no one can really destroy a people like yours. Outwardly, yes, it can appear to happen. They can be killed, scattered, dispossessed – but that is only the physical aspect of their lives which is destroyed, not the spirit of it. And it is this thing of the spirit that has made your people what they are. Do you follow me?'

He paused, but my head was whirling with the force of the idea he had put into it, and I could not answer him.

'Every single one of you who bowed his head in prayer at the schoolhouse meeting had his share of that spirit,' he went on. 'It showed in Rory Ruadh when he extracted that oath from Alexander Munro and organized your resistance to the evictions. Little Elizabeth Ross shivering at her watch-point on the hill had it. Lachlan Chisholm labouring up the Bodach Mhor with you, Katrine keeping the secret of the Sheriff's change of plan from you, your mother proudly raising her scarred face into view in the court-room, yourself stubbornly setting off for Tain to try and save her at the cost of a hangman's noose round your own neck – you were all showing this same spirit of – well, call it what you will, but I do not think there is any one name for it.

'It owes something to the principles of Christian faith, something to courage, something to a high, unconquerable pride of race. But it all adds up to something that is unquenchable and more enduring than life itself, something that nothing and no one can ever kill. And you, boy, you told the Greenyards story better than you knew when you told it in terms of your own struggle with McCaig and the Sheriff, For somehow, you, yourself, emerged from the scribbled account of that attempt to crush you as a sort of symbol of this unnameable, essential, *indestructible* quality of your people.'

I was looking at him now in a sort of daze. His face was alight with excitement, his eyes sparkling eager into mine.

'So you see you have succeeded, Connal. You have!' he said gaily. 'Do you not believe me?'

I tried to speak but suddenly I found that I was breathless and choking with an elation that matched his own. 'Yes,' I managed the one word at last, looking away from him and saying the word, soft and surprised to myself. Then my eyes came back to his face again, and in a firm, loud voice I repeated, 'Yes!'

The word was just out of my mouth when a sailor's voice shouting, 'Land-ho!' rang out from the mast-head.

'Land! Land!' The cry was taken up from all over the ship and from all points people came running to peer ahead to where the sailor pointed. Katrine broke away from us and ran towards the bow of the ship. Hamilton ran after her, calling out as if fearful he would lose her in the sudden boil of people on the deck, and I ran too, knowing that her break towards the bow must mean that the rest of the Greenyards people were congregated there.

I found them all in a cluster on that part of the deck, except for the younger boys who had climbed on to the lower parts of the rigging and were swinging there in wild excitement at the news. Everyone was talking at the top of his or her voice, no one making sense, no one listening to anyone else. Some of the women were weeping, the tears streaming openly and unheeded down their cheeks. I glanced at Hamilton, wondering what he would make of all this display of emotion, but I could have saved my curiosity for he was holding Katrine as she wept and there was a glisten of moisture in his own eyes.

'There it is!' someone called.

We stared, and saw a thin, dark-blue line on the horizon. The line thickened until it became a heavy smudge of dark blue. Then, very slowly, the smudge altered in outline till we could just make out the contours of still higher land above it. Among the throng of people a woman carrying a baby raised it suddenly high in her arms and cried out:

'There, my son! Take your first sight of the Americas!' and everyone standing around laughed and cheered her and the baby.

190

'It is a pity he is too young to speak!' Ian Mackenzie shouted. 'He could be calling a greeting to the Americas for us!'

'It is the pipes we need for that,' a number of people called out. 'Away you and fetch your pipes, John Ross!'

'I'll do that!' John Ross pushed his way out of the crush to go below-decks for his pipes, but Ian was still taken with his idea of calling a welcome. With a great thump on the shoulder to me, he shouted:

'Here is one who never thought to see the Americas at all! Up on the rigging with him and let him be the first to call a greeting!'

A shout of approving laughter went up, and hands seized on me from all sides. I was swung in the air against a blur of cordage and spars, and panic-stricken, I reached out to clutch for a hold on them. My hands closed round a spar, and the hands holding me guided my feet to rest safely on the bulwark. Still fearful, I hung tightly to the spar, but as the wind caught me I felt a sudden flood of exhilaration sweep over me.

I looked down on to the deck. Scores of faces shining with laughter and goodwill were upturned to me, and as I swayed above them in the wind I felt my spirits lift still higher so that I echoed their good-natured laughter.

I was looking forward after all – forward to the new land, to new life, new hope, and the dark, bitter injustice I had left behind me no longer seemed so important. I freed one hand to wave down to Katrine and Hamilton smiling up at me, and then, cupping the hand round my mouth I called out to the Americas the old, old greeting of Greenyards:

'Failte duibh! Sith gun rob so!'

The sound of my voice sped loudly over the waves, and by some trick of the ship's position, a faint echo of it came back to us like a voice quietly whispering the soft, slurring sound of the Gaelic syllables.

'Did you hear that?' an awed voice said as I jumped down

191

from the rigging. 'That answer was an omen – a good omen for us!'

Hamilton put his hand on my shoulder. 'You Highlanders,' he said, smiling towards the woman who had spoken, 'you are all so superstitious!'

I stiffened, ready to burst out with an angry retort, but the pressure of his hand on my shoulder was friendly and the smile on his face was a teasing one.

'Aye, well – maybe,' I conceded, and might have said something more if John Ross had not burst out with his pipes at that moment. It was a reel he was playing, a wild, magnificent, ranting reel-tune that would set any Highlander's feet tapping. Hamilton clapped his hands over his ears at the sound, but Katrine caught his arm and pulled him with her into a group of people forming themselves up into a set ready to step off into the dance.

I grinned at his discomfiture and stood for several minutes longer watching his clumsy attempts to partner Katrine in the light, twirling movements of the reel. The boys who had been swinging in the rigging hooked an arm each round a strut to keep their balance and beat time with their hands for the dancers. They shouted to me to join them and I leaped on to the bulwark, balanced myself, and joined in with the rhythm of their clapping.

We laughed a great deal over the difficulties of keeping our balance like this. I laughed louder than any of them, for I had even greater cause for excitement than they. And so it was like this, laughing and beating time to the music with the rest of the boys of Greenyards, that I sailed into the new world of the Americas.